W9-AQE-958

# "Barb, Please Wake Up!"

How God helped a couple through their daughter's accident and long recovery from a nearly fatal auto accident.

Roy B. Zuck



VICTOR BOOKS
a division of SP Publications, Inc.

Scripture quotations are from the King James Version unless indicated otherwise. Other versions quoted include *The New American Standard Bible* (NASB), © 1971, The Lockman Foundation, La Habra, California; *The New International Version: New Testament* (NIV), © 1973, The New York Bible Society International; *The Living Bible* (LB), © Tyndale House, Wheaton, Illinois. All quotations used by permission.

Library of Congress Catalog Card Number: 76-5688
ISBN: 0-88207-653-1


Printed in the United States of America

VICTOR BOOKS
A Division of SP Publications, Inc.
P.O. Box 1825 • Wheaton, Ill. 60187

Dedicated with warm appreciation to
Dr. J. George Handley and
Dr. Renato Imaña, skilled neurosurgeons
of Central DuPage Hospital, Winfield,
Illinois, and to the many other doctors,
nurses, and therapists
who attended our daughter Barb
during her long hospitalization

## Contents

# 1
# "Barb's Been in an Accident!"

At 5:40 P.M. I drove into the alley behind our house in Dallas, Texas. It was Friday, the end of the first week in my second semester of teaching at Dallas Theological Seminary. As soon as I pulled into the garage I knew something was wrong. My wife, Dottie, was standing at the door leading from the garage to the utility room. She obviously was anxious for me to get home. I opened the car door and asked, "Is something wrong?"

"Barb's been in an accident!" Dottie blurted. "The hospital called about 5 o'clock."

I quickly turned off the ignition, grabbed my briefcase from the back seat, and hurried around the back of the car to my wife. At first the thought entered my mind, "It can't be too bad. Perhaps a broken leg or arm?" But that uninformed thought crumbled when I got inside and Dottie explained the phone call.

"A nurse from Central DuPage Hospital called long distance to say Barb is in the emergency room." Tears welled in Dottie's eyes and the words tumbled out. "She received severe head injuries in an automobile accident and is unconscious. The nurse—her name is Mrs. Beardsley—said the doctors need our permission for them to take an arteriogram, a test to determine if there is a blood clot on the brain. I told them you would be home in a few minutes and would call right back. Then I called the seminary to see if you were still there, but you had gone—that was 40 minutes ago. . . . Where have you been!"

I could see that Dottie had suffered a long 40 minutes. I pulled her close to me, and explained I had stopped at a stationery store to get a pen refill and some greeting cards. I wished now that I hadn't, but there was no time for wishes.

"Do you have the number of the hospital?"

"Here. It's 312-653-6900."

I dialed the number in Winfield, Illinois, 30 miles west of Chicago and adjacent to Wheaton, our hometown for many years. Soon I was talking with Mrs. Beardsley, the nursing supervisor.

"We need your permission in order to proceed immediately with the arteriogram. The doctors are preparing now. If you fly up here to see her, you can sign a permission form when you arrive. Otherwise you should send a telegram immediately. You should be aware that some risk is involved in an arteriogram, but it is minor compared with the information gained for proper diagnosis. Dr. George Handley, our chief neurosurgeon, is in charge of her case and he will call you as soon as he has the results of the test."

"When will that be?"

"In about an hour."

"You certainly have our permission to proceed. We won't send a telegram. Either my wife or I will get a flight to Chicago as soon as possible."

The next hour, between 6 and 7 o'clock, was long and hectic. The three of us—our son, Ken, then 15 years old, was home—discussed several questions: Whom should we telephone? Which of us should fly up? Where would we stay in Wheaton? What about Ken? Could someone stay here with him?

Ken's response to the last question was typical of a maturing tenth grader. "I can stay by myself. Why would I need anybody to come over?"

"Well, you're right," I responded. "If Mom and I both go up, we'll be gone just a few days. And Cookie will keep you company." Cookie is our blond Labrador retriever-cocker-beagle.

"I'll call American and Braniff to see if we can get a flight later tonight," I said, reaching for the phone.

Both airlines told me all flights to Chicago were cancelled because of heavy fog. "The fog should lift by morning," I was told. So I made reservations for a 7 A.M. flight.

As I grabbed a bite to eat, I looked at the clock on the kitchen wall. It was 6:45. "Dr. Handley should be calling any time now." I looked at Dottie. She couldn't eat. She could only think about our 17-year-old daughter and the pending call from the doctor.

At 7:10 the phone rang. I answered it quickly, a

pen and notepad ready. As Dr. Handley talked, I took notes. It was clear to me immediately that he knew what he was talking about.

"The arteriogram showed no blood clot, so it appears we will not have to operate. (That was good news.) The left side of her brain is swollen, apparently from the impact of the accident, and this is related to her unconsciousness. She is being given Decadron, to help reduce the swelling. She is not in a deep coma. There are various levels of unconsciousness, and she is in what is called a stupor. She has no response to verbal commands, but she does have some movement in her arms and legs."

As we began packing, several long-distance calls came. The news was spreading. One was from Warren Benson, a close friend in Wheaton, then on the faculty of Trinity Evangelical Divinity School. Warren offered us a room in his house. How kind of him and his wife, Lenore. That answered the question as to where we would stay. He also told us he had been to the hospital and talked to Brad, the boy who was driving the car.

"How did the accident happen, Warren?" I wanted to know and yet I didn't.

"Brad told me he put his foot on the brakes and his car fishtailed into the next lane and hit a school bus. Barb was sitting in the front right seat and was knocked around by the impact. The car was demolished. The fog was extremely thick here this afternoon. Brad told me he could see only about half a block ahead. He is quite shaken up by it all."

"Was he or anyone else hurt?"

"He has two cracked ribs. He went to the hospital

in the ambulance with Barb, and was treated and released. No children were on the school bus, and the bus driver was not injured."

Later Don Nelson, a neighbor in our Wheaton days, called to say he had heard about Barb, and wanted to know what he could do to help. He insisted on meeting us at O'Hare Airport the next morning.

Another phone call came from Jim Anderson, the warmhearted administrator of Central DuPage Hospital, and a personal friend. He too assured us of his concern and his prayers for us and Barb.

* * *

As we packed our suitcases that Friday night, January 18, 1974, I reflected on the previous weeks. Six months earlier we had moved from Wheaton to Dallas, where I was to become assistant academic dean and assistant professor of Bible exposition at Dallas Theological Seminary, my alma mater. It was exciting for all of us—except for Barb, that is.

Barb did not want to move. She hated the thought of leaving her friends behind and taking her senior year in a new school. We had moved to Wheaton in 1959, when she was three and Ken was one. Both had been born in Dallas when I was a student at the seminary. I received a master's degree in theology and finished my residence work for a doctorate, then accepted the position of editor of youth programs at Scripture Press in Wheaton. Six years in that work was followed by eight years as director of Scripture Press Ministries, a foundation promoting Christian education. The invitation to teach at my alma mater was a new challenge. I weighed the decision carefully, knowing the move would be hard on Barb. But the Lord seemed to say, "Go."

As soon as we arrived in Dallas on July 1, 1973, Barb talked about flying back to Wheaton to visit her friends. I told her, "You need to realize the Lord has led us here. You can make friends as soon as school starts. Going back now would only delay your adjustment to Dallas."

Months passed rapidly with my invigorating responsibilities at the seminary. But Barb was not herself. She was glum and quiet rather than her usual cheerful, outgoing self. She made a few friends at school, but she still talked frequently about Wheaton. At year's end she suggested going back in January between the fall and spring semesters.

"I've saved up money from my job at J.C. Penney's, so I'll pay my own way. I have a week and a half between semesters, and I don't want to sit around here with no snow and no friends."

"I'll think about it," I said. Maybe it would be OK for her to go.

On the evening of January 9 she flew from Love Field to Chicago. She was to return Sunday afternoon, January 20. The accident happened on the 18th, at 3:46 P.M., less than 48 hours before her scheduled return.

She had called us two days before the accident, excited about the good time she was having, seeing friends and teachers at Wheaton Central High, chatting with adults and teens on Sunday at church, staying each night at a different girl friend's house and engaging in chatter and laughter till the early morning hours.

Now the good times were over, and who knew what lay ahead? I folded another shirt and placed it in the suitcase. With a mixture of regret, disgust, and grief, I thought to myself, "If only I hadn't let her fly back to Wheaton!" But that, too, was a part of God's plan.

After a time of prayer, committing the entire burden to the Lord, we got into bed to wait out the night and hopefully get some sleep. "Dear Lord, please keep her alive; we love her so much. . . ."

# 2

# The Long Saturday

The night was short: the alarm went off at 4:30 A.M. We had no difficulty getting up as we were anxious to be on our way.

The ride on the Surtran bus to the new Dallas/Fort Worth Airport was long and dark. Love Field was so much closer to our home, but Barb had taken one of the last flights out of Love Field and was to have returned to the new airport. Now she was lying in a hospital a thousand miles away, unconscious. *Lord, why should this be happening to us?*

The airport seemed eerie at six in the morning. The world's newest, largest air terminal was almost lifeless. Or did it echo our own feelings?

Shortly after nine we landed at O'Hare in Chicago. Our former neighbor was there to meet us, and he took us through the suburbs we remembered so well directly to the hospital.

At 10:20 we put our suitcases in the lobby of the hospital and asked the receptionist where we could see Barb Zuck. Up the elevator to the second floor and around two turns, and we were at the ICU (Intensive Care Unit) door. We knocked. Our hearts were pounding, not knowing what Barb would be like.

This was all unfamiliar territory. No one of our immediate family had ever been hospitalized—except when Dottie brought Barb and Ken into the world. We had never been inside an Intensive Care Unit. A nurse answered the door. We introduced ourselves, and she asked us in. Just then Dr. Handley walked in, introduced himself, and assured us Barb was doing as well as could be expected.

We walked over to Barb's bed. What a shock to see her with a tube in her nose, an intravenous needle in each arm leading to an upside-down bottle hung on a rack, and a tube in her mouth which was attached to a machine that gave her humidified air. In addition, a machine at the foot of the bed kept her mattress cool, thus bringing down her fever.

Overcome with grief and shock, we both felt weak and had to sit down. Dr. Handley continued to talk with us, explaining the situation.

About 11 A.M. Barb was wheeled from the Intensive Care Unit for a test on her kidneys. Meanwhile several friends had already come to see us. It was such a comfort to see them again.

At noon Jim Anderson, the hospital's administrator, took us and his wife, Karin, to the hospital cafeteria. While we were eating, someone called him to the phone. He came back to our table and said it was for me.

"This is Dr. Handley. We are sorry to report that Barb is now losing ground. The medication is not reducing the edema (swelling) in her left temporal lobe, and various symptoms indicate that surgery is necessary in order to reduce the pressure on her brain. The situation is very serious and requires that we operate immediately to remove the left temporal lobe where the swelling is prominent. We will be ready for surgery in about an hour."

I walked back to the table, pleased by Dr. Handley's competent tone but alarmed that surgery would be necessary. Dottie cried when I told the news to her, Jim, and Karin.

It was now obvious that Barb's condition was far more serious than I had originally supposed. "Remove the left temporal lobe," the surgeon had said. How would that affect her mental abilities or her psychomotor functioning? Would she be permanently paralyzed in some way? Would she be in a vegetative state for the rest of her life?

Like giant rats, those questions began to gnaw at my mind. But I kept them to myself, not wanting to add to Dottie's fear. And yet I realized she was probably thinking similar questions.

I had heard of patients who had undergone brain surgery, some suffering serious impairment and others little or none. What would be the outcome of Barb's surgery? We would not know for several hours, maybe even weeks.

Silently I prayed, "Lord, why should this happen to us? I don't understand it. It seems so unnecessary. But I have trusted You with my soul for salvation from sin, and I know that I can also trust You in every problem, whatever its magnitude. Barb is in Your hands."

Jim insisted we go to his office where Dottie could rest. As we walked there, I sensed again how wonderful it is to be a Christian, to have the assurance of eternal life because of my sins having been forgiven by God's grace. How grateful I was that Barb had trusted Christ when she was a young girl. This meant that whenever she would die (which possibly could be in a few hours) she would immediately be with God.

Coupled with my sense of peace was the realization that in all likelihood a comparatively small number of patients and their relatives around me had this assurance, because so few people have a personal relationship with the life-giving Son of God. How tragic that in our Bible-rich country the multitudes know and believe so little of God's Word that they are not prepared to die—at 17 or 70!

Dottie and I were surprised at the number of friends who stayed with us during the entire five hours of surgery. Their presence expressed their Christian love, and we were greatly strengthened by their concern. I had to confess to the Lord that I had never done that for anyone. Now that I knew how much it meant, I would seek to share the blessing in the future.

As I waited through the hours of surgery, I thought about my teaching courses on the poetical and prophetic books of the Old Testament. In three days, I was due to begin teaching, of all things, the

Book of Job! Was the Lord preparing me to understand Job's suffering more deeply before I taught that Book?

True, I couldn't identify with Job in the sudden loss of all his wealth and ten children (Job 1:13-18). Nor was I undergoing the physical anguish he bore (2:7-8). But as I faced my daughter's possible death or permanent injury, I knew something of the throbbing ache in Job's heart. And I, too, had to turn to God.

The surgery began shortly before 1 P.M. and at 5:15 we still had not heard from the doctors. Dottie and I and the others went to the hospital cafeteria, not that we felt like eating, but we knew we should have some nourishment. At 6 o'clock Dr. Handley and his associate Dr. Renato Imaña walked into the cafeteria, looking for us. They called me aside and gave me their report.

They had found and removed a five-centimeter hematoma (blood clot) in the left temporal lobe. It was not on the surface of the brain, immediately under the skull. Instead it was intracerebral, within the brain. The arteriogram test the night before had not revealed this clot. When they found it, as they were removing an area of dead brain tissue, they decided it wouldn't be necessary to remove the left temporal lobe.

Dr. Handley commented, "This should remove the pressure that the swelling was putting on the medulla [brain stem], which connects the brain with the spinal column."

I went back to the table where we were eating and reported what I had learned. One of the group said, "Let's pray and thank the Lord for what He's done."

When he finished praying, I wept. Out of relief —and yet out of grief that Barb had to undergo such an operation. I hadn't wept for years. I felt embarrassed, but I couldn't hold back the sobs. An arm—I don't know whose—over my shoulder silently reassured me that my grief was not being carried alone. "Lord," I prayed silently, "this hurts. But I know You're with me and Dottie and that You'll see Barb through. Thank You for Your goodness. She could have been killed instantly in the accident."

After the surgery it was difficult to watch Barb again entangled in tubes. But, of course, they were maintaining her life. In addition, her head was now bandaged with a dressing that reached down to her eyebrows. A small drainage tube led from her skull through the bandage to drain off excess blood.

That night as we fell into bed, we were exhausted and grieving, but thankful that we, and especially Barb, were in God's sovereign and loving care.

The night before had been short, but that Saturday was the longest day I had ever known.

# 3

# Week of Uncertainty

The next morning Dottie and I woke up early, anxious to get to the hospital to see how Barb was doing. It was January 20, the day she had planned to return to Dallas. Her arrival home was to be a pleasant birthday present for me. But now things were vastly different. Now the important thing was the condition of our precious 17-year-old.

She was doing a little better, the nurse told us. Her blood pressure was good, and she seemed much more relaxed.

That week at the hospital, each day was long and wearying. We could go into the Intensive Care Unit for only ten minutes every hour on the hour. Between these visits we sat in the small 8′ by 10′ ICU waiting room. Or we walked the long hall or sat in the lounge at the end of the hall.

That Sunday, a visitor from the Evangelical Free Church, the church we had attended in Wheaton, told us that in the morning service the pastor prayed earnestly for Barb's recovery, and that our good friend Dr. Louis Barbieri sang a solo, "God Leads His Dear Children Along," selected specifically because of Barb's situation. Many in the congregation had been in tears, sympathizing with us in our burden.

I also learned that the day before, a number of young people gathered at the church for prayer during the entire time of surgery. In addition, some of them stayed at the church throughout the night, continuing in prayer. Said the youth director, "The high schoolers are deeply touched by Barb's injury. As one of them observed to me, 'It could have just as easily been one of us.' I've never before seen them pray so earnestly and with such unity."

This was a remarkable demonstration of the truth of Paul's words about the unity of the church, the spiritual body of Christ: "If one member suffers, all the members suffer with it" (1 Cor. 12:26, NASB). Months later several pastors or laymen were to tell me how the news of our daughter's injury pulled together the people in their congregations in a spirit of diligent prayer.

That morning in ICU a nurse handed us a sack and asked us if we wanted "Barb's hair." That was a shock, especially to Dottie. It hadn't occurred to us that all her hair had to be shaved off for the surgery. The nurse informed us, though, that each month it would grow about half an inch.

That Sunday evening Barb's temperature and blood pressure were normal, but her hands were cold and pale. Dr. Handley said, "According to the book, she should wake up in 72 or 96 hours—three or four days, but of course she hasn't read the 'book.'" That would mean she would be unconscious until Tuesday or Wednesday, if all went well.

That evening we called several relatives, including our son Ken. Dottie asked how he was getting along as a "bachelor." "Do you think Grandma Zuck should come stay at the house? She could cook for you." He responded, "Maybe that would be nice." Apparently two days of cooking were plenty!

That evening Dottie had difficulty going to sleep. She got out of bed, went downstairs to the kitchen and read in the Bible. She turned to Psalm 57:1, part of which states, "Yea, in the shadow of Thy wings will I make my refuge, until these calamities be overpast." She did not know that she would find it necessary to turn to this verse repeatedly for months to come. Later she remarked, "That verse, along with Psalm 61:4 ('I will trust in the [shelter] of Thy wings'), was like my very breath. There was no way I could have kept going without the Lord sustaining me by those verses."

The next day Barb's eyes were in a roving gaze. It seemed as if she might be following us with her eyes, but the doctors said she wasn't. They told us, "She is doing reasonably well, but her condition is still serious and dangerous."

That Monday morning she was taken to the operating room for a tracheotomy, an operation in which an incision is made into the windpipe in order to insert a small tube. Then a masklike apparatus can be placed over the portion of the "trache tube" that protrudes out of the throat. The masklike apparatus is connected by a tube to a machine that supplies humidified air to the lungs. By this arrangement, the air reaches the lungs more quickly than through a tube placed in the mouth, and protects against pneumonia. Little did we know what complications would develop.

A nurse loaned me a book on surgical nursing procedures; I was curious to know what they were doing to my daughter! According to the book, many persons who have surgery in the left temporal lobe become aphasic, that is, unable to express themselves or to understand verbal communication. This prospect discouraged me more than anything else has.

That day Dottie's sister and husband and two boys drove from Muscatine, Iowa where he is a pastor. How good to see them, even though they could stay only until the next evening.

On Tuesday Barb seemed to be about the same, except that her hands were not so cold. She resisted the nurse when her blood pressure was taken—a welcome indication of response. That evening I learned that Barb had been prayed for in the Wheaton College chapel service. Later that week we heard of other groups where people were praying for her: Scripture Press, TEAM (The Evangelical Alliance Mission), Youth for Christ, Dallas Seminary, Moody Bible Institute, Wheaton Christian Grammar School, and Biola College. Word reached us that people in England, Germany, Spain, Mexico, Guatemala, and Australia were praying.

Over the weeks the list of such groups, including churches, grew to more than 100. Such extensive prayer support buoyed us tremendously. I thought of the verse, "Bear ye one another's burdens, and so fulfill the law of Christ" (Gal. 6:2).

One of the visitors on Tuesday was Sung Jin Ahn, a Korean whom I knew through Scripture Press. He is engaged in children's work and in the publishing of Christian literature in Korea. He said to me in faltering English, "How can I console you?" We sensed his Christian love reaching across racial and national lines as he prayed fervently with Dottie and me in Korean!

Though Barb was unconscious, we talked with her about her friends, the weather, and Ken. Perhaps she could hear us but was unable to respond. So we kept on talking! We urged her to wake up soon so that we could go out to eat a steak, her favorite food. As we talked, we rubbed her legs, feet, and arms. But we could not bear to stay long beside her bed; our hearts ached to see her in that condition. The sight was discouraging, but I constantly reminded myself and Dottie of the Lord's omnipotence, His power to do the difficult, even the impossible. "The Lord . . . is great in power" (Nahum 1:3).

On Thursday Barb's condition worsened. She was running a high fever, and there were other symptoms that caused the doctors to think another blood clot may have developed in her brain. Therefore they gave her another arteriogram. Surprisingly, no blood clot was revealed. Her condition continued to be puzzling for two or three days.

Instead of waking out of her unconsciousness, she was showing signs of regression at times and signs of improvement at other times.

Saturday evening Dr. Handley talked with me at length about the situation. He concluded that she probably had a blood clot at the side of the brain stem, a problem that would not show up on any test, but a condition that is very dangerous.

He explained it this way: "The brain stem is a small but extremely vital part of the central nervous system. It is so vital that any pressure against it or any shift in its position can be fatal unless corrected immediately. An operation near the brain stem is risky—it is possible that the operation itself could cause some brain damage. On the other hand, if we do nothing, the struggle will soon be over.

This explained why Barb had not awakened during the week. Now we faced a second lengthy surgery, even more hazardous than the first. Dr. Handley explained that there was definitely a possibility that she would *not* pull through the surgery, though her youth was an advantage.

I asked him, "When do you want to operate?" He said, "I'd like to do it right now, but I'd rather wait till the morning for two reasons: she might improve during the night, and we will all be more alert in the morning."

That night as I walked to the parking lot to get the car loaned to me, the dreary, cold weather seemed to match the weariness of my soul. Like other nights that week, I was chilled, tired, and hurting inside, and I found that tears came easily to my eyes.

Never before had I known the heavy feeling of parents whose child is injured, faces surgery, or is dying. Now I knew. Now I could reach out to others and say, "I understand how you feel."

Never before had I felt much concern about the physical needs of others, it being a foreign experience to me. Now my heart could reach out to them along with my hand. That must be one reason the Lord brought this crisis into my life.

On Sunday morning, the 27th, we were apprehensive. Would Barb pull through? Or was this the end?

The operation began at 10:30 A.M. This was a posterior fossa craniectomy—a cutting into the brain from behind at the base of the skull. I learned later that a Sunday School teacher in Wheaton and another in Dallas stopped at 10:30 in the middle of their classes and led their members in prayer for Barb.

"Lord," I prayed alone, "if You want to take Barb to Yourself during this operation, that will be hard on us. But we want Your will. She would be with You in the glories of heaven, which Paul said is 'far better' (Phil. 1:23). In fact, Lord, if she doesn't pull through, that will be easier on her and us than having her impaired in some way for the rest of her life. But, Lord, have Your way. We love You because You first loved us—and we are dependent only on You."

Amazingly, I had a sense of genuine peace during those trying hours. By knowing Jesus Christ personally, I knew that even death could not separate us from His love (Rom. 8:38-39). How precious to have the assurance that all things—including this—"work together for the good to those who love (God), to those who are called according to His purpose" (Rom. 8:28, NASB).

Only four weeks before, on December 30, I had preached on this passage from Romans 8 at the Pantego Bible Church in Arlington, Texas. I remember saying in that sermon, "Whatever the Lord has brought into your life in 1973 or whatever He will bring into your life in 1974 will be in full accord with His plan for your good and His glory."

Now the Lord was giving me the opportunity to experience that scriptural truth in my own life.

Two visitors that afternoon were Kathy Stephens and her father. About a year before, Kathy, a teenager, had been thrown from a horse and was unconscious for 13 days. Now she was a picture of health and joy. It was so encouraging to see what the Lord had done for her in answer to the prayers of her Christian friends. But that did not fully answer the uncertainty that churned in our hearts that afternoon.

When I had said good-bye to Barb on January 9 as she left for the airport, she half-jokingly remarked, "I may not come back." But I knew she was half-serious too. In her disappointment over leaving her friends in the north, she had let us know she was very dissatisfied and wanted to get away. Our first months in Dallas acquainted us with the conflict that many parents experience with rebellious teens.

In those months my wife and I prayed earnestly that the Lord would remove Barb's bitter attitude.

I asked Him to use whatever means were necessary to accomplish that purpose—with no inkling of what it might take. That recollected prayer haunted my mind during the second operation.

Also tugging at my heart that afternoon were Barb's words, "I may not come back." Was that to be true? Would she not recover from this operation? All I could do was commit her again to the Lord.

At 2:15 P.M. the phone rang in Jim Anderson's office. "This is Yvonne Freshour in the Operating Room." My heart flipped. Dottie sighed tensely. Across my mind flashed the question, "Is she calling because the battle is over or because Barb is OK?" Mrs. Freshour was the surgical nurse, whom we had also known at our church in Wheaton. The Lord had put so many wonderful people on the case!

"Dr. Handley asked me to call you and give you a report. We are a little more than halfway through and Barb is holding her own."

Holding her own. What wonderful news!

Mrs. Freshour continued. "They did find blood on the brain and it has been removed. Dr. Handley will give you more details later. We can't say that we have won yet, but we are making progress."

I hung up the phone and reported the news to Dottie and the others who were waiting there to hear the outcome. Dottie cried tears of relief.

The surgery was completed at 3:45. Dr. Handley reported later that diffuse blood was on the surface of the cerebellum (the "motor control panel" of the brain) and on the occipital lobe at the back of the brain. In addition, there were extensive contusions (bruises) on both sides of those areas of the brain, which would take a long time to heal.

"It may be weeks before she becomes conscious. We don't know exactly how long—maybe six weeks, maybe 9, or 12, or 16."

We were beginning to realize we had a long vigil ahead of us—if Barb recovered from this second surgery. The week of uncertainty was over, but more testing lay ahead.

# 4

# Scrambled Flight Plan

The days following the second operation moved slowly, each with its own highlights. The following excerpts from the diary I kept illustrate them:

*Tuesday, Jan. 29.* Barb's right lung collapsed. This could be causing her fever of 102°. Her right eye is more open, but her arm and hand muscles are tense. (The other day Bob Murfin announced Barb's condition on WMBI—Moody Bible Institute's radio station—and asked listeners to pray and to send cards. Sixteen cards came today from WMBI listeners, all of them from people we do not know.) Dottie is exhausted. I had her stay at Benson's today instead of going to the hospital.

*Wednesday, Jan. 30.* I had Dottie rest at Benson's today too. Barb moved her left leg today. Her lung problem is now gone. She seems more relaxed. We received 31 cards today from WMBI listeners.

*Thursday, Jan. 31.* Barb is restless again. We received 11 cards from WMBI listeners—58 in three days. I'm amazed. Lord, You are so kind to us.

*Friday, Feb. 1.* Dr. Handley had the nurses put Barb in a wheelchair with the back reclined. This was her first time out of bed in two weeks, other than for the surgeries. I flew back to Dallas for a week, leaving Dottie and Barb in Winfield. I had to finish editing the seminary catalog, and care for other business. It was good to see our son Ken again. And how good to pray with him on our knees beside his bed.

*Saturday, Feb. 2.* Dr. Handley said, "We are encouraged about this young lady. She is going forward, but it's by millimeters, not inches. Even though she has involuntary movements of her arms and legs, her other signs are good."

*Sunday, Feb. 3.* Barb moved her head to the side on her own. A small thing, but encouraging.

*Monday Feb. 4.* The doctor said he is thinking of moving Barb from the Intensive Care Unit to a room on the hall.

*Tuesday, Feb. 5.* Dr. Imaña (Dr. Handley's associate neurosurgeon from Bolivia) said Barb followed him with her right eye when he walked to the other side of the bed. (Her left eye is still closed.)

*Wednesday, Feb. 6.* Dr. Handley asked Barb to stick out her tongue and she did! He told Dottie, "That may not seem like much progress, but take my word for it. It is very significant." Barb was anemic today. Was given two pints of blood.

*Thursday, Feb. 7.* Barb was terribly restless. When reclining in the wheelchair, she slid down repeatedly. The nurses secured her with sheets, but they weren't completely effective. Dottie noted: "The nurses are so wonderful to allow me to stay in ICU as much as I want. But it is hard to see her like this for very long at a time. Sometimes I or a nurse push Barb in the wheelchair a short distance in the ICU in order to give her some motion. After supper I went back to the hospital. Barb is still extremely restless. I feel so depressed. It has been a hard week being here without Roy."

*Friday, Feb. 8.* I flew back to Chicago.

*Saturday, Feb. 9.* The nurses gave Barb a bit of orange marmalade on her tongue to see if she would swallow it. She did, which means she has the swallowing reflex, controlled by the brain stem.

*Sunday, Feb. 10.* We took our unconscious daughter for a wheelchair ride down the hall. Bill, a middle-aged patient who had been in ICU when Barb was, but who was now in a room on the hall, saw her go by. He stood at his door with tears sliding down his cheeks.

* * *

That day as we took Barb down the hall I could not help but wonder about the future. Would I be pushing her in a wheelchair the rest of her life? If not, for how long? She was far from normal. Though the surgeons were not pessimistic, they were hardly opimistic either. Their words of encouragement were cautiously stated. And understandably so. They did not want to build up our hopes only to have them dashed.

Each day I was usually encouraged about Barb's progress, though it was almost immeasurably slight at times. But occasionally the prolonged trauma and uncertain future "got to me." Fortunately, when I was down, Dottie was encouraged. Conversely, when she was discouraged, I was not. In addition to contemplating the Lord's faithfulness and power, we consoled each other by means of the diary I was keeping. It was helpful to read the diary, comparing Barb's condition one day with her worse condition a few days before. These threads of slight progress became cables of confidence and hope.

* * *

*Monday, Feb. 11.* Barb was moved out of ICU to Room 2121, a semi-intensive care room. Dr. Handley spoke about moving her later to a rehabilitation hospital, possibly in Chicago. He talked as if she might need to be there for weeks, even months. I asked when we could consider taking her to Dallas. He said, "Her vital signs are stable, so she could endure a flight in a week or so. If you can arrange it, it will obviously be easier for all of you to have her near your home."

*Tuesday, Feb. 12.* I went into action immediately. I called Braniff Airlines and made arrangements to fly Barb to Dallas the following Tuesday. I also arranged for an ambulance to pick us up at the hospital to take us to O'Hare Airport, and for an ambulance to meet us at the Dallas/Fort Worth Airport to take us to Baylor Hospital.

I also called Baylor Hospital and arranged for our arrival. Dr. Handley was surprised to learn all was ready so quickly. But I was anxious to get her back to Dallas.

*Friday, Feb. 15.* I spoke to the Scripture Press employees in their chapel this morning. I reported on Barb's condition; I thanked them for their concern and tangible help; and I commented briefly on Psalm 18:30: "As for God, His way is perfect." I related how the week before in Dallas I had found a sheet in Barb's desk with the words of the hymn "Security." Then I concluded my chapel message by reading the very meaningful words of that hymn, all the while fighting with a lump in my throat.

More secure is no one ever
Than the loved ones of the Saviour,
Not yon star on high abiding
Nor the bird in home-nest hiding.

God His own doth tend and nourish,
In His holy courts they flourish;
Like a father kind He spares them,
In His loving arms He bears them.

Neither life nor death, can ever
From the Lord His children sever,
For His love and deep compassion
Comforts them in tribulation.

Little flock, to joy then yield thee!
Jacob's God will ever shield thee;
Rest secure with this Defender.
At His will all foes surrender.

What He takes or what He gives us
Shows the Father's love so precious;

We may trust His purpose wholly
'Tis His children's welfare solely.

*Saturday, Feb. 16.* Her hypertonic posturing (tense, involuntary movements of arms and legs) was slightly reduced, but still continues.

*Sunday, Feb. 17.* Barb lifted her head by herself today!

*Monday, Feb. 18.* Dottie packed Barb's things in preparation for the trip tomorrow. Dottie is desperately tired. She kept thinking, "What an awful way to have to take our daughter—but at least we are taking her home."

*Tuesday, Feb. 19.* Flight day to Dallas.

* * *

The nurses spent the morning getting her ready. They washed her hair, now half an inch long. They dressed her in the blue pajamas I bought her the day before the trip.

The ambulance came at 12:20 P.M. to take us to the airport. There were four of us—Barb, Dottie, myself, and Rea Johnson, a part-time nurse in ER (Emergency Room) at Central DuPage Hospital. Rea, a dear friend from our Wheaton days—we used to live on the same block—volunteered to travel with us. In fact, two other nurses also had volunteered to fly with us to Dallas. Airline regulations require a nurse or doctor to accompany a patient being transported on commercial flights. Besides, we knew we needed a nurse; Barb's condition still required constant nursing attention.

As we took the long, silent ambulance drive of 25 miles to O'Hare International Airport, I reflected on the events of the preceding month. What a different chapter this was in our lives—an experience that we would never be able to blot from our memories. But how merciful God had been to spare Barb—and to give us physical stamina and spiritual strength to undergo such a trying 32 days. Dottie told me later that though she was terribly exhausted, the Lord had given an extra measure of optimism and hope, a sense of spiritual calmness in the storm.

In a way, it was difficult leaving Central DuPage Hospital. We had come to know and appreciate our two neurosurgeons and many of the nurses, therapists, and staff personnel. Everyone was exceedingly kind to us. It was especially heartening to have a close bond with several Christian nurses who often assured us they were praying for Barb. What a deep appreciation I now have for medical personnel, for people whose lives are dedicated to helping others. "Thank you, Lord, for their skills and their personal warmth."

Jim Anderson, CDH's administrator, had told us that Barb was known and talked about throughout the hospital. Patients, doctors, nurses—numerous ones frequently inquired about her condition.

I remember going to see Elmer Engeseth, who was hospitalized when Barb was there. I had known him at the Free Church. An elderly, godly Swede, with a warm, loving heart. He was suffering from an ailment that took his life a few months later. Before I could inquire about his health, he insisted on knowing about Barb. Then *he* led us in prayer, praying with tears for her recovery.

Now the ambulance was on Interstate Highway 90. In about 20 minutes we would reach the airport. I thought about what the Lord was doing through this "incident"—not accident!—in our lives. He had given Dottie and me opportunities to share our faith in Christ with several individuals. I remembered the day when a woman and her teenage daughter sat beside us in the ICU waiting room. We introduced ourselves to them, and began talking. She told us her son had been brought to the hospital with head injuries from roofing material whipped at him by the wind on a construction job. Not until a year later did he regain partial consciousness. We told her about Barb's injury and shared what the Lord's comfort means to us.

Then I recalled the woman whose husband was in the cardiac unit with a heart attack. She was tearful and very distressed over his condition. Sixteen days after Barb's accident, this woman said to Dottie, "I've been watching you and your husband for two weeks now. You seem to have such peace. What is it that makes the two of you different?" It was Dottie's joy to tell her about the peace that Jesus Christ gives to those who know Him as personal Saviour. A week later I spoke with her at length about the problem of sin, the gift of God's love, Jesus' substitutionary death for her on the cross, and the way to have forgiveness of sins and eternal life through faith in Christ. I showed her several Bible verses, such as Romans 6:23, "For the wages of sin is death, but the gift of God is eternal life through Jesus Christ our Lord"; Romans 5:8, "But God demonstrates His own love toward us, in that while we were yet sinners, Christ died for us" (NASB); and John 3:17-18, "For God did not send His Son into the world to condemn the world, but to save the world through Him. Whoever believes in Him is not condemned, but whoever does not believe stands condemned already because he has not believed in the name of God's one and only Son" (NIV).

I had also met another woman whose husband was suffering from a serious heart condition. One evening as she walked to the elevator I noticed she was in tears. I asked her if there was anything I could do to help. She said, "No." But I sensed she was in need of comfort. So I got on the elevator with her and rode down the one flight to the main level. She was on her way home, so I walked with her to her car in the parking lot, encouraging her to share her burden. What a burden! Her son was on drugs and was not interested in seeing his sick father, her husband was failing and might not recover, and she was out of money. My heart went out to her. As I stood by her car door in the freezing weather, I told her what Jesus Christ means to me. I shared with her some verses from the Bible about the way to be right with God and to know His joy and peace. She seemed appreciative.

Since then, my wife and I have frequently remarked that we could have maintained a fulltime ministry right there in the hospital, talking with people about the Saviour in their times of need.

As the ambulance proceeded through the traffic, I prayed, "Lord, I don't know if these women have trusted Christ for their salvation, but I pray again that you will bring them to Yourself. Thank You, Lord, for Barb's accident because through it You've enabled us to show the peace that only You can give to suffering people. What a difference You make in a person's life."

The ambulance pulled up in front of the Braniff section at O'Hare. The driver and his assistant wheeled Barb on the ambulance stretcher into the airport as the three of us—Rea, Dottie, and I—followed. What a strange feeling to be wheeling our unconscious daughter down the long corridors at O'Hare. I guess it was only natural for people to turn and stare at us.

Barb was wheeled onto Braniff Flight 31, before the other passengers were allowed to board. The backs of the first two window seats on the left side of the first-class section were pushed forward, thus allowing room for a stretcher-cot to be placed near the windows. Rea sat beside Barb in the first seat next to the aisle, I sat behind Rea, and Dottie sat behind me. (We had to purchase five tickets for the four of us.)

Central DuPage Hospital had loaned us a portable suction machine, which Rea would take back on her return flight. The machine was needed in order to draw mucus from Barb's lungs, a process necessary every hour or so with patients who have tracheotomy tubes in their windpipes.

When I plugged in the machine, it did not work! I asked a steward if he knew of another outlet where I could plug it in. We tried different outlets, but nothing worked.

Now what do we do? Dare we take Barb on the

flight if the suction machine does not work? I had called the airlines a few days before in order to be sure the machine would work on the airplane. I was assured it would. But I did not know that the cycle of electricity on most airplanes differs from the cycle in the suction machine.

I got off the plane—no one else had boarded yet—and went to a telephone booth. I called a medical supply company in Chicago to see if they had a rentable suction machine that would work on the airplane's electricity cycle. They didn't. So I asked a policeman if he could help me. He called the airport's emergency fire squad, but they could not help me either.

I was getting frantic!

I went back onto the plane. The flight engineer had been told of our plight and had come out of the cockpit to see what he could do. Before becoming a pilot he had trained to become a medical technician, so he was somewhat knowledgeable of the situation. He suggested that we could possibly suction Barb by inhaling at one end of the suction catheter, thus creating a vacuum. It was clear that this was our only choice.

The ticket agent had come onto the plane and was anxious to get the flight on the way. I could understand his concern, but yet I wanted to be sure that we had some way of suctioning Barb. She would be off the humidified air system for several hours before we could get her to Baylor Hospital, and if the mucus were to get too dry and clog her trachea, she would die.

The rest of the passengers boarded, and we took

off at 3 o'clock—one hour after the scheduled departure time. Already Barb had been without humidified air for two and one-half hours. The flight would take two hours and then it would be another hour or so before she would be in the hospital at Dallas. *Lord, this is a difficult situation. But You know about it. Please see us through.*

The stewardesses on Flight 31 were helpful and concerned. One who was particularly helpful was Mrs. Barbara Ehlers of Kansas City. Dottie remarked later, "I don't know how we could have made it without her loving attention." Interestingly, a few weeks later Mrs. Ehlers telephoned us at our home to ask about Barb. She also said the flight engineer had called the hospital several times to inquire about our daughter.

Barb was very restless during the flight. Unconscious, yes, but constantly jerking her legs and arms, and obviously uncomfortable. She constantly scooted down the cot, requiring Rea and me to pull her back up every few minutes.

Caring for her in that way reminded me of the many times years earlier when each night Dottie and I tucked in our Barbie, as we called her then. Those bedtime moments are precious to every parent. And especially to Christian parents who seek to instill biblical standards in their children in the early, impressionable years. Those quiet moments are ideal for praying together, talking together, sharing, and reading.

The plane landed in Dallas about 5 o'clock. I was glad to see the ambulance drivers at the gate. They were ready to move Barb to the ambulance.

One of my pieces of luggage was among the last to come down the baggage chute—another disturbing delay.

When we arrived at Baylor Hospital, a mixup in communications resulted in our taking Barb to the wrong place. Finally we got her situated in a room in the rehabilitation center, and a resident doctor examined her thoroughly. Her lungs were extremely dry from lack of humidified air for six hours. The center did not have adequate nursing staff to watch her constantly as required, so we hired three private-duty nurses, each for an eight-hour shift.

The next day, Wednesday, Barb was moved to another section of the hospital, but not to the neurological unit because no beds were available there. Therefore she was in a room a long distance down the hall from the nurses' station, making it difficult for the nurses to give her the steady attention she needed. So we were forced to hire more private-duty nursing care. We began to wonder: Had we done the wrong thing in bringing Barb to Dallas? How could we continue to pay almost $100 a day for round-the-clock private nursing care in addition to all the other costs? We were at our wits' end.

# 5

# Barb Wakes Up!

Bill Webb was God's answer to our dilemma.

Bill is an elder at Reinhardt Bible Church where we are members. Somehow he heard about our situation and he came to the hospital to explain his solution. "The elders want to sit with Barb during the evenings and nights. This will relieve you from having to pay private-duty nurses."

And what a relief it was! Bill's offer was most welcome. He set up a schedule of three-hour shifts for the elders (and in some cases, their wives too) and others to sit with Barb. Dottie and I were deeply touched by their sacrifice. Our new sitters watched Barb, called the nurse when she needed to be suctioned, rubbed her legs to calm her from her periodic thrashing, and talked to her. These actions were some of the suggestions Dottie had written on a list of instructions for the sitters. Marsha, a neighbor who sat with Barb, was surprised to read on the instruction sheet: "Talk to Barb as much as you'd like." Marsha's reaction was, "What do you say to an unconscious person?" Then she continued reading: ". . . in order to give Barb as much audible stimulation as possible to help her wake up."

On February 20, my wife wrote in our diary, "Barb seems so aware. She looks up with her right eye at the T.V. when it is on. We show her many of the cards we've received—more than 300 now—and we talk to her even though she is only semi-conscious and has no way to respond to us. We keep rubbing her legs and putting lotion on her. *Oh, dear Barb, please wake up! We love you so!*"

Much as we were deeply grateful to the elders and others for being with Barb, I knew we could not continue with that arrangement indefinitely. We needed to get Barb in a situation where her room would be nearer a nurses' station. I discussed the problem with our doctor and we agreed that the best solution would be to transfer her to Presbyterian Hospital of Dallas—if we could get her a room in the neurological unit. That hospital would be much closer to home—two and one-half miles, compared with Baylor's seven and one-half. I made arrangements on Friday, February 22, and on Monday at 1 P.M. we took our third ambulance ride in seven days.

Even today, the wail of an ambulance siren makes my heart palpitate as it jolts my memory of those agonizing days. But every siren has become for me God's "signal" for prayer. I hear an ambulance siren and I pray for the patient being attended, and I praise the Lord again for what He has done for our Barb.

Barb's room—number 947—was directly across from the nurses' station, which was ideal. It was bright and spacious, with a large picture window looking north. This was to be Barb's "home" (and our "second home") for the next 93 days, till May 29.

On February 25, we had no idea what the future would hold. We wondered how long she would remain in her partially conscious state. We wondered if she would ever be able to walk or talk again. We wondered if she would ever be able to feed herself. In fact, as the days dragged on, we frequently pondered, "Lord, how long?" and "Lord, why this terrible ordeal?"

On the other hand, we knew we have a great God who had said, "Is there anything too hard for Me?" (Jer. 32:27) We were confident that He who made the human body with all its intricate systems —and especially the brain—could also heal it.

We also recognized that God's will might be for Barb *not* to be fully restored. Our prayers could not tell God what to do. They had to be voiced in an attitude of willing submission to His best plan for our lives. I believe I was honest when I prayed, "Lord, if You will receive glory to Yourself by Barb being a cripple in a wheelchair or a vegetable the remainder of her life, then that is what we want. On the other hand, if it is Your desire to restore her, we will glorify You for that."

Those thoughts were voiced a few months later when I preached in the morning service of my home church in Dallas. Before the sermon I reported briefly on Barb's progress and told how God was working through those onerous events, thus making the accident an incident in God's planning. Later Alton H. Wilson, a fellow-member at the church, told me how my words affected him. He wrote this poem* about Barb:

Lord,
I cannot possibly know how he felt.
I can only reach out to him
Father heart to father heart.
His beautiful daughter, a loving high school student,
Was in a grinding auto crash,
For weeks she lay unconscious.
The doctors gave limited hope for recovery,
And the little hope they gave was tempered
with the knowledge
That if she lived it might be in an impaired
mental state.
The friends rallied to their side.
The church prayed.
The parents waited . . . and hoped.
Consciousness began to return very slowly.
She is still speechless, possibly forever.
Her beauty is marred, but life has been spared.
Her father spoke last week in church,
To thank the fold and to inform them of her
progress.
He said, "This incident was no accident."
He spoke of faith, hopes, dreams.

---

* Reprinted with permission of Doubleday & Co. from *Lord, It's Me Again*, by Alton H. Wilson. Copyright 1975 by Doubleday & Co.

And all the while he spoke, Lord,
I was putting myself in his place.
I too have a lovely teen-aged daughter
For whom I have great love and aspirations.
Yet I still have my daughter, fresh,
beautiful, and healthy.
Were mine like his, how would I feel, Lord?
Would I exude hope, or hopelessness?
I hurt for him. I wanted to say "I understand"
But I know I didn't. What could I know?
Only love.
The father heart in me reached out to the father
heart in him,
Though he never knew it,
And I ached, and wept inwardly,
And prayed fervently.
"Like as a father pitieth his children."
Bless that dear man, Lord!
I pray that Your Father love will reach out to
comfort
Not just that father, but all who have been touched
by her life.
The daughter may actually have the easier part.
She is not suffering the pain of a broken daughter.
Thank you, Lord,
For my dear daughter.
I pray that I may never have a burden like his
to bear.
But . . . if I do, help me, Lord,
To bear it in faith and confidence,
Like the example of this father.
Bring glory and good out of "this incident
. . . no accident."

God answered Mr. Wilson's prayer that God would comfort me, that glory and good would come out of "this incident." Others, too, expressed to us their heart-hurt for us. They said they wondered how they would bear up under such an experience if their daughter were involved.

There was a certain aloneness in our situation. Though surrounded with friends, few really knew the depth of the ache in our hearts. And those who did conveyed it more by wordless touch than by paragraphs of attempted consolation.

On Barb's first day at Presbyterian Hospital she slept peacefully all afternoon in her sunny room. It was as if she, too, was relieved to be "settled." How thrilled we were that day to see a slight smile on her face for the first time since the accident. But it was almost a false smile—there was only a slight upturn of the corners of her mouth.

This was so different from most of her years. As a baby she smiled frequently and easily. She seemed to enjoy life. Her bubbly attitude was contagious. She was such a joy to us. Now her forced smile seemed to accentuate the contrast between the girl we knew years before and the girl we now had in the hospital.

One day Dr. Richard North, chief neurologist, called Barb's name and she turned her head immediately and looked at him. We were thrilled to realize she could hear, especially when the surgery into her left temporal lobe was so close to the area of the brain that controls hearing.

Barb no longer needed to be watched through the night, but many friends were volunteering to sit with her during the day. Soon a schedule developed in which Dottie went to the hospital from eight in the morning till two in the afternoon, when someone came to relieve her. That person stayed till 4:30, when I came from the seminary. I covered till seven when another person came and stayed till nine or 9:30. The "sitters" came on the same day and time each week. Many of them were seminary students' wives.

On March 6 we noticed that face pimples—caused, apparently, by the trauma to Barb's system—were less pronounced. Also, she was beginning to swing her right arm all the way over to the left side of the bed. The following week a friend reported that Barb moved her left fingers. Ruth had been praying specifically about Barb's left arm and hand, which were less mobile than her right side. Ruth was so thrilled to see God's answer to her prayers. It was as if our family had enlarged to embrace numerous individuals who were as concerned as we about Barb's condition. On March 13 Barb raised her head and reached up with her right arm to pull the pillow down under her head. How excited we were to see this—a deliberate, volitional action!

The next day Barb's tongue was sticking out between her teeth and when Dottie told her to pull her tongue into her mouth, she did! Two days later the nurses found that Barb had pulled out her bladder catheter, and the next day she tugged at the humidified-air tube leading from the wall above her bed to the masklike cover over her "trache tube." She was obviously trying to get rid of this unnatural apparatus that "tied" her to the wall. Dr. North explained that all this was a good sign—an indication of increased awareness. In addition, Barb was lifting her feet over the side railings on her bed, trying to get out. For several weeks afterward it was a continual task to keep her calm and to prevent her from falling out of bed.

Sunday afternoon, March 17, Dr. John Hannah, a faculty colleague at Dallas Seminary, was sitting with Barb. He phoned us from the hospital to report, "I have some encouraging news. I am quite sure that Barb's left eye opened slightly today."

Indeed, it *was* encouraging news. This was the first indication of any "life" in that eye since the accident. For about three weeks her right eye had been fixed on objects or had followed moving objects, but the left eye had remained closed. March 17 was the beginning of a three-week period in which her left eyelid opened a little more each day.

A few days later Barb pulled out a third tube—the N/G (nasal-gastric) tube, which leads through the nose down the esophagus to the stomach. It was through this tube that she was given liquid food several times each day. The tube had to be reinserted, of course, but the next day she pulled it out again. Consequently the doctor told the nurses to leave it out and to begin feeding her orally. She seemed to be ready for oral feeding because two days before that she had been given some water from a cup and had eaten some ice cream.

But still the question haunted me. Would she ever recover to the level where she could feed and care for herself? It was now more than two months since the accident, and she had such a long way to go to recovery. She could not walk or talk or care for herself in any way. Nevertheless the progress she had made in her first month at Presbyterian Hospital showed that God was healing her. She had come from her semiconscious condition to full consciousness; her left eye had opened and her left hand began to move; her limb movements were more voluntary; and she began to eat orally. Praise the Lord!

# 6

# Rending The Veil

From almost the first day after Barb's injury, physical therapists gave her "range-of-motion" therapy. This was to prevent her muscles from becoming atrophied. Her arms, wrists, fingers, legs, feet, and toes were massaged and moved repeatedly twice a day.

On March 14, Mrs. Firra, head of the Physical Therapy Department at Presbyterian Hospital, and two other therapists worked on getting Barb to hold up her head while lying in bed on her stomach. They explained that this was the first step toward restoring a fully coordinated use of her muscles and regaining her ability to stand and, hopefully, to walk. In fact, Barb would need to go through all the stages of muscular development and coordination a baby goes through, involving a kind of repatterning of the muscles and of the brain cells that control muscular movement.

The steps would include holding up her head, sitting up, balancing herself while on her hands and knees, crawling, kneeling, and eventually standing, and—perhaps—walking. Mrs. Firra explained that this process usually takes months with brain-injured patients like Barb who have been unconscious and immobile for weeks.

But not so with Barb. In only 18 days she progressed through all the stages! On March 14 she was holding up her head while lying on her stomach in bed and on April 6 she was walking, though falteringly, without holding on to anyone!

That was our Barb—always quick to learn, eager to move ahead. She had always been a good student in school. Her report cards in the lower grades invariably had more V's (Very satisfactory) than S's (Satisfactory), in upper grades more A's and B's than C's. Learning to ride a bicycle, to read, to play the violin and piano, to swim, were easy attainments. She was active in school, in the church youth choir, in summer camp, in high school events.

She never lacked friends. Even as a preschooler her outgoing smile made her popular. In high school our telephone got such constant use I expected the telephone company to triple the amount of my bill!

Each day Barb was taken from her hospital room to the Physical Therapy Department on the basement level. The therapists worked with her for almost an hour at a time. Some days she was in P.T. (Physical Therapy) in both the morning and the afternoon.

Occasionally I went with Barb to P.T. to watch how they worked with her. I had become fascinated with the field of medicine. A whole new vista of knowledge had opened before me. Reading about the brain, talking with the neurosurgeons, watching nurses and therapists at work with Barb presented a panorama of interest that still intrigues me. In fact, these experiences brought to mind the times when in high school I had seriously considered becoming a missionary doctor.

As I watched the therapists put Barb on a mat on the floor, I realized again how grateful I was for hospitals and medical personnel. Without them, my daughter probably would not be alive today.

The therapists put Barb's knees under her stomach, moved her elbows under her shoulders, and propped her up so that she was on "all fours." But she tipped over; she was unable to stay in that posture by herself. However, in only a few days she was not only steadying herself on her hands and knees, but was crawling on her hands and knees for 20 feet. At this time she also developed the ability to sit up in bed by herself.

It was pitiful in a way to see her movements limited to those of a healthy infant. I thought of the times when she played doctor as a six-year-old, examining her brother Ken's heart with a toy stethoscope as he lay "sick" on the floor. Now *she* had regressed to childhood functions—temporarily?

P.T. helped Barb develop such psychomotor skills as putting on her slippers, buttoning her pajamas, sitting up in a chair, getting up from the mat to a wheelchair, catching and throwing a large beach ball, opening a cabinet door. There were many motor activities, however, that she could not do: dress herself, walk steadily, walk backwards, go up and down stairs, or run.

In P.T. she was asked to play tic-tac-toe on a chalkboard. I was thrilled to see that she remembered how to do it. But I was disappointed with Barb's answer when the therapist asked, "How old are you?" Barb wrote on the chalkboard, "11." Later that week, however, I asked her the same question, and her response was "16." That was better, but still not correct. So I told her she was 17, and from that time on she had it right.

At times she balked at going to P.T. We did not understand why she should resist the help, then we realized she was becoming nauseated by the exercises. The reason for the nausea was not clear. Later the answer became evident: because her left eye was open, though still damaged, she was seeing double, which in turn was causing dizziness and nausea. The answer was to have her wear an eyepatch. It was not until August—four months later—that she could leave the eyepatch off without feeling dizzy.

Another thrilling moment in her recovery came on Wednesday, March 27. The day before, she had pulled a pencil from my shirt pocket and made a babyish scrawl on a pad of paper, "Lord," I prayed, "I do hope the day will come when she can write again."

That prayer was answered within 24 hours. Wednesday afternoon she again took the pencil from my shirt pocket and motioned with it as if she wanted to write. I placed a 4″ x 6″ pad of paper on her lap as she was propped up in a sitting position. She put the pencil to the paper, and I fully expected her to scribble again as on the previous day. But, she printed the letter *M*. Then the letters *I*, *K*, and *E*, thus spelling the word "Mike." I could hardly believe my eyes! This was her first tangible communication with us for ten weeks (other than nodding her head for yes and shaking her head for no—which she also began to do that same day).

She continued printing. On four slips of paper she printed these words:

M-I-K-E
V-I-C-K-I-E
A-R-E T-H-E-Y
C-H-R-I-S-T-I-A-N-S ?

The letters were wobbly and unbalanced, and some were almost illegible, but I knew what she was spelling because I watched intently as she made each letter. Her words looked like the printing of a three- or four-year-old first learning to print his name.

Excitedly I picked up the phone and dialed home. Dottie answered the phone. "Guess what Barb just did! She printed! Isn't that wonderful?"

"What did she 'write'?" Dottie asked.

I told her what Barb had written, and added, "How thrilling to realize that she has mind-hand coordination, that she has memory recall, that she can spell correctly, and above all, that she asked about Mike and Vickie's spiritual welfare!"

Mike and Vickie were high school friends of Barb's who had been dating for some time and were contemplating getting married. That explained Barb's sixth printed word: "Married?" She wanted to know if they were married yet. She printed only six more words that day, two of which were "Ice cream." So I got her some ice cream. Then when she wrote "Hurt," I asked her if her throat hurt, and she answered by writing "Yes." Her two other words were "Ice" and "Wet."

To Dottie and me, March 27 was a turning point in Barb's recovery. It was remarkable that she did not ask first about herself, such as, "What am I doing here?" or "What happened to me?"

Barb's printing that day was her first deliberate verbal communication since the accident. It was evident that she was fully conscious, having emerged from the mental haze that cloaked her perceptions so long. Once again, she could communicate with us—the veil was gone!

I like to think that her interest in Mike and Vickie's faith was the result of our efforts to provide spiritual training for her earlier years. As soon as we had learned that Dottie was pregnant, back in the early part of 1956, we dedicated to the Lord our to-be-born baby. Two years later we did the same with our son Ken when he was "on the way."

We knew that becoming parents would be an awesome responsibility. We were aware that we must bring up our children in a certain way, namely, "in the discipline and instruction of the Lord" (Eph. 6:4, NASB).*

Soon after each of our children was born, we again dedicated them to the Lord, privately at

---

* In this verse the word *discipline* is literally "training" or "education"; and the word *instruction* means "verbal direction," including warning, counseling, correcting.

home and publicly in a Sunday church service. We encouraged them to respect the Bible, to love the Lord Jesus, to pray to God, to help others, to seek to be like Jesus, to enjoy going to church. We read and told them Bible stories, we saved their Sunday School take-home papers and frequently read them together. Later we encouraged them to attend Bible camp, to become involved in the church youth group and youth choir, to memorize Scripture, to have their own personal devotions, to share the Gospel with others, to give of their income to church and missionaries.

As parents, we found that "dinner talk" was an excellent way to instill biblical concepts and Christian standards. The informal atmosphere of eating together somehow makes it easier for these matters to be discussed. Not that we discussed them every day. But when we did, it was natural and positive. When our children were in elementary school, we talked at dinner about the importance of their marrying a Christian, going to a Christian college, choosing the right kind of friends. By giving a biblical perspective to their experiences, they were helped to see life from God's point of view.

In family worship we stressed the value of prayer—praying for others in need, thanking the Lord for Himself and His goodness, adoring Him in worship. One fall, we were driving through the Morton Arboretum, near Wheaton. The sun, shining through the multicolored leaves, made them glisten with a breathtaking beauty. As we commented on God's visual display, little Barb suggested, "Let's stop and thank the Lord for the leaves." We got out and stood ankle-deep in the freshly fallen leaves to thank the Lord for His creative goodness. It was a precious moment of family worship.

That event was a year or two after Barb received Christ as her Saviour at the age of five. It was a parental thrill for Dottie to explain the Gospel to Barb, who, we believe, sensed at that tender age her sin and the need for Jesus to forgive her. Many Christian young people and adults have responded to the Gospel in a similar way in their preschool years.

In Barb and Ken's junior high and high school years, I found that one effective way to discuss problems with them was by "car counseling." When I was driving Barb to a friend's house one day, I conversed with her about a problem. This atmosphere was more relaxed, we were not in a face-to-face confrontation, and yet we were together until we arrived at our destination. On more than one occasion, that "environment" has given an excellent opportunity for counseling.

Teen-parent tensions—and what parent doesn't have them?—can be eased to the degree that the parents maintain open lines of communication, pray earnestly for their teens, and evidence genuine concern, all the while treating their teens with respect.

We made a special investment in the spiritual training of our children in August 1964. I had been asked to address the student body of the Central American Bible Institute (now the Central American Theological Seminary) in Guatemala City. We decided that taking Barb and Ken along would give them an excellent opportunity to see a mission field firsthand, and thus add to their understanding of and concern for missions. The many dimes and quarters saved for that trip were well worth the investment in their spiritual development.

The training Christian parents lovingly and consistently provide for their children *does* eventually pay off. I knew that for sure when on March 27 I watched Barb falteringly scribble her deep concern about Mike and Vickie's relationship to Christ.

# 7

# Notes, Games, and Praises

From March 27 on for five weeks, until she was first able to whisper on April 29, Barb wrote steadily. She printed at first, then began cursive writing a few weeks later. The first letters were large, several inches high, and unusually squiggly and uneven. But over the weeks the letters became smaller and neater, and the lines were more evenly horizontal across the page. It soon became time consuming for people to visit her because she slowly wrote out her "conversation."

Not all her writing made sense to us. For instance, on her third writing day (March 29) she printed "You bring tachas." We could not determine what she meant by the word *tachas*. Thinking she might mean she wanted a taco to eat, I drove four miles to a drive-in and brought it back to her. But she immediately pushed it away. *Tachas* did not mean "tacos"! Then we thought she may have been referring to her trache tube because she also wrote "Did you call Dr.?" In fact, it was on that same day that she pulled out her trache tube, and the doctor had to be called in to reinsert it. To this day, however, we do not know the meaning of *tachas*.

Some words were not the correct ones, but we were able to determine what she meant. One day she wrote, "Why do I go to gymnastics?" She meant the Physical Therapy Department. Apparently the walking bars and other therapy equipment looked like apparatus in a school gymnastics room. That same day she wrote to Dottie, "I think I'm dreaming" and "I just might live with you."

I wanted to check her memory on certain things, so I gave her some simple addition, subtraction, and multiplication problems. She did them with no difficulty or hesitation. Then I pointed to parts of my face—chin, nose, mouth, eye, ear—and asked her to write what each one was. She identified them with no difficulty. I asked her to look at my watch and write down the time. It was 4:34, and her answer was 4:36. I was glad it was close. She even remembered how to write shorthand from her school course in it.

On April 2, when she began to stand up by herself in P.T., she wrote to me, "My new legs will come." A few days later she printed what to us was something humorous but which to her was very serious. This was when she was not wanting to go to P.T. because of the dizziness and nausea caused by her left eye double-vision. She printed in large letters on a 8½″ by 11″ sheet of paper: "No basement girls. Go away, you guys," and she insisted that a nurse tape it to the outside of her room door! (By "basement girls" she meant "physical therapists.") The sign was her way of saying she did not want the therapists—or anyone else—to take her downstairs for a physical therapy treatment.

Now that she could write, she began to express her desire to go home. "When I gonna go home?" she printed on her 8½″ by 11″ pad. (She often habitually spelled "going to" as "gonna" This was our Barb!) I told her it might be awhile before she could go home. She would have to wait till she regained her strength. Apparently that answer was not specific enough for her because she wrote, "A few days?" I said, "Probably not a few days," and she then asked, "A couple days?" The next day she brought up the subject again, by printing, "Home today?" Three days later she tried once more. "Are you gonna drive me home?"

Perhaps Barb's room stimulated her longing for home. Each day Dottie had brought something from Barb's bedroom at home—an object that would be familiar to her and that hopefully would bring a response. Her room, several nurses said, was the most cheerful in the neurological unit. We felt this stimulation was important to her recovery.

Another form of visual stimulus we used was the Viewmaster. Barb seemed to enjoy looking at that, even though it was with one eye. Dottie suggested we see how Barb would do at Chinese checkers. We were pleasantly surprised that she had no difficulty at all with the game. So we took Scrabble to her room—and she played it well.

Throughout the month of April she played Scrabble repeatedly—it almost seemed to be a qualification for sitting with Barb! She also amazed us with her ability to check the scorekeeper's addition (even though it was upside down to her) and to correct any miscalculating. Each day increased our expectation that the Lord would restore her completely.

Dottie's mother planned to fly to Dallas from Tucson on April 16 to be with us and to help Dottie with housekeeping. (My mother had returned to Phoenix the month before.) We marked that event on Barb's wall calendar, and at first she thought that was the date when she would be going home. We could tell that even though she was making rapid progress, her mind still played occasional tricks on her.

She began to develop an enormous appetite. As I mentioned earlier, in March she pulled out her nasal-gastric tube twice. She was given liquids and soft foods at first, but she was anxious to have solids. On March 31 she ate half a banana, drank Sprite from the bottle, and ate a peanut butter and jelly sandwich which my wife made at home and took to her. Every weekday, without exception, for the last several years Barb's lunch menu had been a peanut butter and jelly sandwich. Now she ate the smuggled sandwich with great delight. The next day she ate her meals while sitting up in a chair—another "first." Her desire for her other favorite foods soon came back—including steak, and butter and crackers. The latter was her favorite snack. We kept the nurses busy supplying Barb with butter and crackers from the hospital kitchen.

In eight days her enormous April appetite helped her regain 13 of the 20 pounds she had lost during her hospitalization. I remember taking her for a walk down the hall one evening at 8 o'clock after she had eaten a large dinner. When we returned to her room she printed on her notepad, "What's there to eat?"

At our house we pray as a family before each meal, giving thanks to the Lord for the food and praying about other matters too. I suggested to Barb that we pray before she ate. She serenely bowed her head. From that time on, before every hospital meal, she would fold her hands and motion to me to pray.

In April and May she seemed so docile, so agreeable. Her cheerful, sweet attitude contrasted remarkably with her bitterness during our first six months in Dallas. She was now more like her former self. What a blessing—at what a cost! I could not understand why God had permitted all this, but remembering the patriarch Job, I was not about to argue with God.

Job went astray at that point. Though his extensive suffering was undeserved (contrary to what his friends dogmatically and heartlessly asserted), Job quarreled with Him and even insisted that God report to him. He asked God, "What have I done to Thee? . . . Why hast Thou set me as Thy target? . . . Let me know why Thou dost contend with me. Is it right for Thee indeed to oppress?

. . . I will argue my ways before Him. . . . I would present my case before Him and fill my mouth with arguments" (Job 7:20; 10:2-3; 13:15; 23:4, NASB).

Job's three friends had said he was suffering because he had been sinning. However, this rigid theological view—that suffering is always the direct result of some specific sin—did not fit Job's experience. God Himself had told Satan twice that Job was "a blameless and upright man, fearing God and turning away from evil" (Job 1:8; 2:3, NASB). Job's problem arose when he let his pain lead him to demand an answer or explanation from God. Rather than suffering because he was sinning, he was sinning because he was suffering. For this reason, he needed to repent and receive God's blessings (Job 42:6).

We may be suffering in a way that seems undeserved and unfair. But to insist that God offer us an explanation is to doubt God's goodness and question God's sovereignty—His right to be *God* over all.

We may wish God could accomplish His purposes in less painful ways, but our complaint is useless. For, as God asked Job, "Shall he that contendeth with the Almighty instruct Him?" (40:2). After God revealed to Job His sovereign lordship over nature, Job confessed his own insignificance and acknowledged that "Thou canst do all things, and . . . no purpose of Thine can be thwarted" (42:2, NASB). For Barb and for us, her parents, I know that God was accomplishing His purposes through His actions. I praise Him for His revelation that "as the heavens are higher than the earth, so are My ways higher than your ways, and My thoughts than your thoughts" (Isa. 55:9).

One day in April Barb asked a nurse in writing to call Dottie at home. She wanted Dottie to bring something from home to the hospital. Then it occurred to Dottie that we could communicate with Barb over the phone by her tapping out answers with a pencil against the phone. We agreed on a system of signals. We would ask yes-or-no questions, and Barb would answer yes by tapping the phone once and no by tapping it twice. When we would tell her good-bye, she would say good-bye by tapping it several times. But not only did we call her; she called us. She would "tell" us, "Hi, this is Barb," by breathing heavily. This was a strange experience, but we were delighted it was Barb—and that she was breathing.

Those weeks, from approximately the middle of March to the middle of April, were filled with exciting progress. She could now walk, eat, read, play games, and recall events in the past. Mary Coffey, one of Barb's nurses, told me, "I've been in neurosurgical nursing for two years and Barb's recovery is the quickest and most complete I've seen in a patient with her kind of injury."

After bringing Barb to Dallas I had written to Drs. Handley and Imaña regularly, giving them reports on her progress. In response to one of the reports, Dr. Handley wrote, "Everyone is quite elated over Barbara's progress, since we have so many young people do just the opposite."

We were beginning to appreciate the unusual

nature of Barb's speedy comeback. But new problems shadowed the progress—some *serious* problems.

# 8

# "Dad, I Love You"

It wasn't until April 5 that Barb began to inquire in detail about the accident. Prior to that time I had told her in general what had happened—that she had been in a car wreck, that she got knocked around in the car, that she was unconscious for two months.

Now she wanted to know more. "What happened to me? Was anyone else hurt? Were there children on the school bus? Were there witnesses? How long have I been in the hospital? Will I be normal? When can I walk? When can I talk? Am I a senior? Why was I in Wheaton?"

After getting her questions answered, she began to respond emotionally to the fact of the accident. She wrote, "I don't like being this way." "I hate the accident." "I look terrible." "I hope I won't remember the accident."

There appears no chance that she will ever recall the accident. In fact, she does not remember anything about her first eight days in Wheaton prior to the accident. Somehow the events on those eight days did not get imbedded in her long-term memory cells. Her memory of events prior to her Wheaton trip is unaffected. She still recalls happenings from her childhood and high school days with the same vivid detail she always possessed. It is clear that the memory cells related to those long-term events were unaffected.

The first week of April marked remarkable mental progress for Barb, but also some frustrating physical problems.

My wife's sister and her husband—Keith and Ginny Sorensen—came to Dallas that week for a pastors' conference. Their church in Muscatine had prayed earnestly for Barb's recovery. We told Barb they were coming to visit, and we didn't discover until after they were gone that Barb thought they came to see her because they feared she was going to die.

Somehow the possibility of death was in her mind that week. One day she printed on her pad, "I want to die." The next day she printed, "Everything hurts," and "I'm going to need glasses." The following day she wrote that her left eye hurt her all day, but I was pleased that she added, "I don't want to die."

Barb was becoming aware of the future prospects as well as present surroundings, and she found some things disturbing.

"What is causing her diplopia (double vision)?" I asked Dr. North.

He explained that one or more of the three cranial nerves (in addition to the optic nerve) that lead from the medulla (brain stem) to the eye were damaged. This may have been caused by the injured left temporal lobe pushing against those nerves. One nerve (cranial nerve III—the oculomotor nerve) controls four of the six eye muscles, some of which may have been weakened by the nerve damage. A change in the tension of the eye muscles can cause the images not to fall in line, thus causing double vision.

In March two other problems had become evident One concerned her left arm. The physical therapists noticed that her left arm was inflexible at her elbow joint. She had good movement at her shoulder and in her wrist and fingers, but her elbow was locked at a 90° angle.

An X ray of her arm revealed that ossification (growth of bone tissue in a muscle) had developed just above her elbow. This condition often develops in patients with injury to the brain or the spinal cord.

When I asked how the problem could be solved, an orthopedic surgeon said surgery would be necessary to remove the bone tissue from the muscle, but that it should not be performed until at least eight or ten months after the accident. "In that period of time," he explained, "the ossification process continues. Surgery performed before the process is complete would need to be repeated later."

This was a problem Barb would have to live with until the fall, at least. This, however, was minor when compared with the more serious permanent injuries she might have suffered.

At the time the arm problem became evident, another—and more serious—problem arose. The otolaryngologist (ear, nose, and throat doctor) changed Barb's trache tube to a smaller size. This was to be the first of several changes to smaller sizes, so that eventually the tube could be removed altogether. However, the doctor said that when he inserted the smaller tube he sensed some kind of obstruction in her windpipe. He did not seem troubled by the problem, and yet something was wrong.

A few days later he checked Barb and decided he should take her to the operating room for an examination. He found and removed some growth tissue from within the windpipe immediately above the trache tube. Evidently this scar tissue had grown in an effort to get rid of the foreign material, the trache tube. The tissue had completely closed her trachea above the tube, which meant that without the trache tube she would have no way of getting oxygen. Obviously this was a life-or-death matter.

This surgery, though, did not permanently solve the problem. It was only the beginning of a long series of eight surgeries on her trachea over the next four months.

The otolaryngologist and the thoracic surgeon who teamed with him had reported that the granulation tissue could grow back. If it did, they would consider transplanting a skin graft to the inner lining of the trachea.

And the tissue did reappear. In only 23 days Barb was back in the operating room. A few minutes before she was taken on a stretcher to surgery, she asked me to pray. As we went down the elevator with her at 2:30 that afternoon, she was smiling! She was cheerfully anticipating the surgery as a step toward being able to talk. That was our cheerful Barb!

In the surgery, they decided against a skin graft. Instead, they inserted a hollow cylinder to hold the trachea open and possibly to prevent granulation tissue from closing the trachea again. This meant she now had two inch-long objects protruding from her neck!

Two days before that operation, Dottie went to the hospital in the morning and I came in the afternoon. When I arrived, Dottie said to me, "Barb has a surprise for you." Then with a big smile Barb *spoke* to me! "Hi, Dad. I love you."

I was so excited and surprised! I hugged her tightly. Those were her first words in three months. Then she demonstrated two more words: "grape popsicle." I say "demonstrated" because it was not normal speech. She was learning to force air through the trache tube and up past her vocal cords, while she covered the trache tube with a piece of gauze. It took practice to coordinate the expelling of air with the movement of the vocal cords and the covering of the tube.

At first, then, the words were only whispered consonants. And more than a week passed before she felt like doing more whispering.

Her talking, though only a whisper, was especially encouraging to us for two reasons: (1) The blood clot in her left temporal lobe was dangerously near the speech-control area of the brain, thus creating the possibility, though slight, that she would have speech difficulties the rest of her life. (2) The granulation tissue which was growing in her trachea was less than an inch below her vocal cords, thus dangerously close to her speech mechanism. We thanked the Lord for this additional answer to prayer in her recovery.

# 9

# Home Again

One day in April as Barb was becoming more alert, she pointed to the ceiling. It looked to us as if she were pointing to the examination light, recessed in the ceiling above her bed. We were puzzled as to the meaning of her gesture. Wanting that bright light on seemed a bit strange.

"Do you think she wants that light on?" I asked Dottie.

"I don't think so, but I'm not sure what she is trying to communicate."

"Well, let's turn it on and see."

I flipped the switch on the stand near her bed, and the bright examination light came on. Immediately Barb motioned to me to turn it off. It was apparent that her pointing to the ceiling was not a request for that light.

In her frustration she printed, "I think I'm dreaming," and "heaven."

"Oh, that's what she means," I concluded. "She thinks the light is heaven."

But a few days later she pointed to the ceiling again and wrote, "Zero is the stuff you take to die."

Now I was more confused. What was "zero"? Was it a medicine? And why would she connect the ceiling with zero?

These questions raised serious ones in my mind: Are her thinking processes impaired? Is she having difficulty functioning intellectually and expressing herself verbally? My heart was heavy with the thought that we might be forced to try to decipher the meaning of "zeroes" and ceiling lights the rest of our lives. Yet I was comforted by the fact that she was now making steady improvement—even though it seemed so slow.

More than a week went by before I got a partial answer to the "ceiling mystery." Barb wrote to me, "I went to the angels' place once."

Angels' place? She must be referring to heaven. So I said, "Barb, maybe you dreamed it. Tell me about it."

Her response was interesting. "I might've dreamed it, but I can't tell you about it."

I asked, "Why not? Is it difficult to describe?"

She dismissed the subject by answering only my second question with a mere yes.

Months later I asked her again about her going to the "angels' place." She added some information about her "dream." She mentioned that she saw Jesus and numerous angels who escorted her toward her Grandpa Zuck (my father who died in 1968) and Grandpa Blythe (my father-in-law who died in 1967). She commented that heaven was indescribably beautiful.

To this day several questions remain unanswered: Was there any connection between her pointing to the ceiling and her dream of heaven? When did the dream occur? If it occurred at the time of the accident, why does she remember only that? Or if it occurred at the time she was coming to full consciousness, why should such a dream occur then?

I have discussed these questions with Barb, and neither of us knows the answers. Perhaps we never will until we can talk it over with Jesus in heaven.

However, this dream (or should it be called a vision?) remains in Barb's mind as a very special and precious thing. Occasionally she has said, "I am anxious to go to heaven," or "It would be wonderful to die and be with Jesus." Death holds no fear for her.

My wife and I have talked about the fact that relatively few young people—and adults, too, for that matter—can say they are ready to die. Only the Christian with assurance of salvation can confidently face death, knowing he will be with Jesus Christ.

Satan holds unbelievers "all their lives . . . in slavery by their fear of death" (Heb. 2:14-15, NIV). "The sting of death is sin," Paul wrote (1 Cor. 15:56). By this he meant that death has a sting, an undesired hurt, because humans are sinners. When a person turns in faith to Jesus Christ for forgiveness of sins, God gives him the gift of eternal life and removes that fear of death. In him is "forgiveness of sins, in accordance with the riches of God's grace" (Eph. 1:7, NIV). Death, then, for the Christian, while usually not desired, can hold no fear because it is the "door" through which the believer passes en route to an eternity of fellowship with God.

When Jesus was on the way to Lazarus' grave, Martha, a sister of Lazarus, went to meet Jesus. Jesus told her, "He who believes in Me will live [i.e., have spiritual life eternally in heaven] even though he dies [physically]" (John 11:25, NIV).

We are grateful that Barb does not fear death but is instead anticipating heaven.

Only three days after Barb told me about her dream, she almost died. That evening a nurse suctioned Barb in a routine procedure. It had to be done several times a day, almost hourly, in order to remove mucus from her bronchial tubes and trachea. If the mucus is loose and made moist by the humidified air apparatus, it is easily removed. If the mucus is dry, it is more difficult for the suction catheter to remove it.

As the nurse operated the catheter, she sensed something was wrong. The dry mucus was clogging Barb's trache tube. And with a clogged trache tube, Barb had no airway. Without leaving the room, the nurse called for a doctor from the emergency room. Within seconds, the room was swarming with doctors and nurses—perhaps ten or twelve altogether.

The doctors worked frantically, for they knew that if Barb were without oxygen for three or four minutes many brain cells would suffer irreparable damage. Barb's life was in their hands! Within a minute and a half, the doctors cleared the trache tube and Barb's breathing was restored.

Dottie and I did not learn about this till the next morning. The crisis had occurred at 10:30 P.M., an hour or so after we had gone home. Dr. Greenlee, associate neurologist with Dr. North, told us in the morning what had happened. He said he did not call us at home because he did not want us needlessly to lose a night's sleep.

He assured us that the problem would not recur. He had ordered the humidified air to be kept on her much more frequently. Though she was still to be "on the mist," she had been "off" it for too long a time, thus creating the dry mucus problem. The doctor also increased the frequency of her IPPB (Intermittent Positive Pressure Breathing) treatments. Each treatment was given by a respiratory therapist to help open the small air sacs in the lungs as a precaution against pneumonia.

That day Dottie and I thanked the Lord for bringing Barb through another near-death crisis. As an EEG (electroencephalogram) therapist told us that day, "She has passed so many hurdles."

Two days before this crisis was Easter Sunday. Dottie went to church and I went to stay with Barb. When I arrived in her room, she wrote, "Happy Easter. It's too bad you're not going to church." We had an interesting morning together. We watched a church service on TV, prayed together, and listened to a cassette, *Jesus Is Coming,* recorded by the Wheaton Free Church choir. While listening to the cassette, she wrote, "That's pretty." A moment later she wrote, "They're good."

As we talked, I told her again that many people had told me personally or had written to us that they were praying for her. She printed, "Thanx [her usual spelling] to them."

Not only was she interested in spiritual things; she also displayed her sense of humor. A man in the room next to her was coughing frequently and Barb wrote, "I can hear that sick man next door barking." Realizing that her left side was more stiff and immobile than her right side, she printed, "I gotta work on this whole side. Yuck!"

That Easter Sunday afternoon we received permission from the doctor to take Barb outside in a wheelchair. We wheeled her out the front lobby and down the sidewalk in front of the hospital. She enjoyed it immensely. She had her pad and pencil with her, of course, and wrote, "It's fun seeing little kids. I like being outside."

Then she began thinking about the coming summer. Several times she expressed interest in going swimming, getting pizza, and going to Six Flags Over Texas, an entertainment park. She even mentioned going to summer school to catch up on the schooling she was missing.

When discussing Barb's accident with her one day, I was delighted that she wrote, "God has a purpose in everything. I know that He caused the accident." It was encouraging to me that she was recognizing God's ability to use what may seem like a tragedy to bring glory to Himself and to accomplish His purpose.

Later in May she wrote to a friend, "I think

about God a real lot. I'm closer to Him than I've ever been."

Perhaps this is why a respiratory therapist told me, "She's the darling of the hospital. Her courage and faith are seen by all."

Her spiritual progress was also seen in her willingness to try memorizing Psalm 1. I worked with her several times each day, reviewing a verse or part of a verse, and then memorizing another verse or line. She wrote a note about Psalm 1 to one of the many girlfriend therapists she had made at the hospital: "I'm memorizing Psalm 1. It's good for me! I think about it when I wake up at night. Read it sometime." That day when the therapist came to Barb's room, she told me, "Barb never complains. She is always smiling. She's a miracle. A real inspiration to me."

Barb was also progressing physically in May toward the possibility of going home. That would not be possible, the otolaryngologist told us, until he knew if the shunt inserted on April 18 was holding her trachea open and could be removed, along with the trache tube. He—and we—hoped it would be toward the end of the month.

On May 9 Barb was given a pass to go home for three hours, from 1 to 4 P.M. That was my wife's birthday—and how delighted she was with this "present!" Barb's first day home in almost four months was exciting for all of us. All except for Cookie, our dog. She hadn't seen Barb in so long that she wasn't sure she knew Barb. Furthermore, Cookie may have been confused by the fact that Barb was so quiet. Only occasionally did Barb attempt a raspy whisper. She went from room to room, looking in the closets and opening the drawers in order to refresh her memory of home.

The following Sunday was Mother's Day. Barb got to go outside again; this time she was walking and not in a wheelchair. She went outside on Wednesday, too. How she enjoyed the warm sun—and the change of scenery from the familiar hospital room.

The next Sunday, May 19, Barb had another pass, this time two hours in length. She wanted us to drive by her high school and other familiar sights she hadn't seen in four months.

Wednesday, the 22nd, was a day she was anticipating. It was the day her trachea shunt was to be removed. For weeks she had felt embarrassed about the two "ugly" things sticking out of her neck, so much so that she had hung a towel over the mirror on the cabinet door in the bathroom so she wouldn't see herself.

In the operation the surgeons found that the shunt, in place for five weeks, had not prevented granulation tissue from growing. The tissue merely grew below the shunt. After the surgery—her eighth time under anesthesia since the accident—the IPPB treatments were given only four times a day, and were discontinued during the night.

The following day Barb wrote to a friend, "God is miraculous." She was increasingly aware of God's protective hand on her. That night I asked her to pray. She put her finger over her trache tube and whispered, "Dear Jesus, thank You that I'm OK now. And thank You for today and for tonight.

Amen." That sweet, simple prayer voiced through a trache tube, brought tears to my eyes (as it does even now as I write these words).

Barb was relieved to have the shunt removed, but even more excited to have her trache tube removed (simply pulled out by the doctor in her room) on Saturday, May 25. What a sense of victory came to our hearts to see the therapist "dismantle" the IPPB machine and remove the suction catheters and related equipment. To think we were finally at the stage where these encumbrances were no longer needed!

Sunday was an especially exciting day. Barb was given a seven-hour pass, from 2 to 9 P.M., and she went to church for the first time since January. So many people at church were delighted to see her! Many said, "Seeing her alive and walking and without brain damage is like seeing a walking miracle!" It seemed that everyone at the church had been in the battle with us. They had prayed for Barb and us, they had sat with Barb at the hospital, they had cooked meals for us, they had sent us gifts: true spiritual brothers and sisters in Christ. And now they were seeing the results of their praying and of their labors of love.

It was interesting to note that many elementary school children were fascinated to see Barb. One even asked for Barb's autograph!

The church service that evening was a special treat. The youth choir presented a fastastic one-hour youth musical on the life of Christ, entitled *Celebrate Life*. Our son Ken was in the choir. So the service was especially meaningful to Barb: she was indeed celebrating life, physically and spiritually.

May 29 was the day we all anticipated with joy. We checked Barb out from the hospital and drove her home, arriving at 10:25 A.M. What a different feeling I had as I drove into the garage, so different from the time I arrived four and one-half months earlier, on January 18. What an ordeal the Lord had taken us through in those 132 days. How utterly exhausting—physically, emotionally, spiritually. But at the same time, how triumphant.

That morning when I talked with the otolaryngologist, a Christian, he said he knew God was helping Barb. He added, "She has been a real inspiration." And when I thanked Dr. North, he replied, "We just stood by and watched."

How true. We all stood by while God worked wonders!

# 10

# Summer Storms

It was exciting to have Barb home. The house had seemed so empty without her for all those months. A typical teenager, she was soon on the phone with her friends, talking now with her natural voice. And that first evening May 29, she went with Ken to our church's youth group meeting. She told us afterward, "Those kids are so nice to me."

She fretted over her appearance, though. Her hair was only two inches long, her left eye still patched, and her left arm was locked in its 90° position at the elbow. And yet her cheerful smile "distracted" people's attention from those problems. They rejoiced with her in what God had done.

But the summer ahead was to be another ordeal. On Saturday, June 1, only three days after her hospital release, we were back in the emergency room!

Barb was having difficulty breathing, not gasping for air, but inhaling noisily. We suspected a return of the granulation tissue in the trachea. If that were the case, her condition could become serious. The checkup was reassuring: "This raspy sound is common after a trache tube has been removed," said the doctor. So we drove home, relieved. But the relief didn't last. She had surgery that Saturday morning and went home Monday.

*Now,* we thought, *the problem is solved.* But we were wrong. A week later Dottie called me in Atlanta, Georgia, where I was representing Dallas Seminary at a conference. "Barb is back in the hospital again! She had to sit up most of last night in order to breathe. So I called the doctor this morning and he had me admit her to the hospital for surgery this evening."

"Will this be the same surgery as last week?" I asked.

"No, he will insert a stent (a cylinder-like tube) in her trachea. He plans to keep this in for six to eight weeks. He hopes that will help hold the trachea open."

"I'll try to get a plane right away. I'll come directly from the airport to the hospital."

The conference was to conclude the next day, so I would miss only a few sessions. I got a flight that afternoon and arrived at the hospital at 6:45, half an hour after Barb was taken to surgery. During the long wait disturbing thoughts went through my mind. Why should this problem have to continue? What was the Lord trying to tell us? Would this stent really work?

I decided to stay with Barb that night and also the next night in her hospital room, sleeping on a cot provided by the hospital. At 11 o'clock Barb wrote a note to Dottie saying she would take care of me during the night and see that I behaved myself. This tenth time under anesthesia hadn't numbed her sense of humor!

During the night she woke up and wrote to me, "This is awful. I feel like crying." She was apparently in some pain, and perhaps discouraged by all the surgeries and this setback of having something back in her trachea (and extending out of her throat about an inch). My heart went out to her; I wished I could have traded places with her.

She recovered quickly, and was released on Monday, June 24. The Saturday before, two friends from Wheaton were in Dallas and went to see Barb. They were amazed at her overall progress, and she told them, "I don't know if anyone has become a Christian through this or not, but if even one person were to accept the Lord I would go through this 50 times."

When we checked Barb out of the hospital, the surgeon told us to put a vaporizer in her room (in order to keep her air moist), and to rent a suction machine and purchase suction catheters so that we could suction her mucus. We had seen nurses suction her several times daily, and now it was our turn. That was a new experience! It wasn't easy to poke a long tube down our daughter's throat, which made her gag every time. But it had to be done.

Three days later Barb was rasping again. Back we went to the emergency room. There the doctor said the vaporizer was not providing sufficient moisture for her lungs. He advised us to rent a nebulizer, which provides humidified air through a tube attached to a masklike apparatus which fits over the trache stent. In this way Barb could breathe the same kind of moisturized air which she got in the hospital.

For all that equipment, Barb's bedroom began to look like a hospital room. For long periods she was "tied down" by the nebulizer. She would sit at a small table and paint wooden decorations for Christmas trees. We had to laugh, though, when she said the vapor puffing from her throat looked like smoke from a dragon.

For ten nights I slept on a mattress on her bedroom floor. That way I was nearby to suction her when necessary or to change the liquid unit in the nebulizer. I began to feel like a nurse and a respiratory therapist combined.

We were still making trips to the hospital for the physical therapy treatments. In June we thought these thrice-weekly trips, along with the two emergency-room stops and the two surgeries would suffice for the summer. But they didn't. On July 9, we took Barb to the doctor's office when she couldn't talk. The doctors concluded that granulation tissue might be growing again—this time possibly over the stent opening. So the third surgery of the summer (and her eleventh since January) was on July 11.

We were disturbed by the postsurgical report: "As we suspected, tissue had grown over part of the top of the stent. We removed it, but we may need to consider inserting a larger stent. We may have to keep excising the granulation tissue as it grows back."

Then they began to discuss the idea of more radical surgery. "A more permanent—but more difficult—solution is to remove the damaged portion of her trachea which keeps collapsing. Then in order to pull the trachea up so that we can reconnect it, we may need to make incisions into each lung and loosen up the bronchial tubes. Or we may need to consider sending her to a surgeon in Boston, who has recently developed a variation of this surgical procedure."

Our hearts sank! Another surgery. Possibly another trip. That day we prayed, "Lord, we don't know the end to all this. But we know You know and You care for us. We pray that she will not need the more serious surgery, and that she won't need the trip to Boston. But we want to be in Your will and to be willing to follow Your plans for us. Lord, we feel so helpless. But we look to You, and we thank You for Your love and comfort."

We took Barb home that afternoon. This time she had been in the hospital only seven hours in the "day surgery" unit.

At supper the next day I noticed that the protruding part of the stent in Barb's windpipe seemed bent. It looked as if it had possibly been broken off. Again I called the surgeon. He suggested we meet him at the emergency room. When he looked at it, he concluded, "The only thing we can do is to remove the stent and put a trache tube back in." He was beginning to doubt that the stent was helping the trachea stay open, anyway. He arranged for an operating room and an anesthesiologist, and he replaced the stent with a trache tube. At midnight we drove her home.

My thoughts were dark. We seemed to be regressing, not progressing. Barb had a trache tube again, the stent was not helping, and no solution seemed in sight other than a long trip for major surgery.

That weekend I thought deeply and I prayed earnestly. Then I moved into action. I felt it might be time for some additional medical advice. A total of seven surgeries over four months, not counting the initial tracheotomy, had not helped her windpipe one bit. I knew, though, the surgeons were trying to avoid more radical surgery.

I told a good friend, Dr. John Binion, an internist, about the situation, and asked his advice. He suggested we contact Dr. Donald Paulson, an experienced thoracic surgeon in Dallas. Monday I contacted Dr. Paulson and he said he would be glad to see Barb. The next day, we were in his office, right across the street from the seminary!

He looked at the list of Barb's surgeries which I had written out, and then at her throat with the trache tube in it. Then he looked at us and said, "Frankly, she has no choice but to have major surgery, a primary anastomosis, to remove the weakened portion of the trachea and to reconnect it. It will not be necessary to go into the lungs." He said he had performed this kind of surgery for 25 years.

Immediately I felt confident about the prognosis. He explained that she would be in the hospital for about two weeks, including several days in Intensive Care after the surgery. He emphasized that without this operation she would continue to need a trache tube and surgeries to excise the tissue growth. Though we didn't relish another surgery, I thanked the Lord for the answer. This could be the final operation on her trachea.

Only four days later—Saturday, July 20—Barb was admitted to Baylor Hospital. Surgery was scheduled for the following Wednesday, giving the doctor several days to have extensive X rays and tests made.

On the 24th she was taken to the operating room at 7:15 A.M. That day was Dottie's and my twentieth wedding anniversary. That was an unusual and unsettling way to spend an anniversary—sitting for several hours in the waiting room near the Intensive Care Unit. It was an agonizingly long wait; time went slowly.

At 12:30 P.M., after five hours, Dr. Paulson came to see us. He assured us it was successful, but that it was more difficult than he had supposed. Two inches, rather than three-fourths of an inch, of her windpipe had to be removed. He explained that he also sewed her chin down to her chest! This was to keep her from lifting up her head and thus pulling against the stitches in her trachea until they could heal.

At 2:10 we went into the Intensive Care Unit. It was painful to see Barb again with a tube in each arm, a tube in her mouth leading to her lungs, her chin sewed to her chest, and groggy from the anesthesia. She was uncomfortable for several days after that, but her vital signs were good. Dottie or

I could visit her for only ten minutes every other hour, so we took turns. Two days later, when the endotrachial tube was removed, Barb pointed to her mouth (to show me the tube was removed), and she clapped.

She progressed quickly. Soon she was talking, playing Scrabble, then sitting up in bed, then walking. On Monday, she was moved to a room "on the floor," and on Tuesday her chin-to-chest surgical thread was removed. She was glad to be able to look up as she walked, rather than holding her head down.

Nine days after the surgery we took her home. We were deeply grateful that this problem had at last been solved. These two months had been wearying for all of us. Yet, they were also times to trust the Lord.

# 11

# End of the Tunnel

That summer was a mountain range of problems. Each time we scaled a peak we found ourselves confronted by another. And they continued, into the fall. We began to wonder, where's the end?

One problem was the six-inch scar from the surgeon's incision in Barb's neck. This necklace-like scar was like the mouth of a "Have a Happy Day" face—about a third of a complete circle. It was immediately below another scar, silver-dollar in size, where the trache tube and shunt had been. These two scars began to keloid, that is, to thicken above the surface. Surface scars can be hidden by cosmetics, but thick, lumpy scars can't be hidden so easily.

A September visit to a plastic surgeon indicated that surgery could not remove her keloiding, but the injection of cortisone directly under the scars might reduce it some. After a series of such injections over several weeks' time, the scars did flatten out to the surface.

A second problem was Barb's left eye. The earlier examinations in August, September, and November 1974 indicated that the left cranial nerve III was injured, resulting in double vision, constant pupil dilation, and some damaged eye muscles. In August 1975 her eye was examined once again. This time the conclusions were similar: Surgery cannot correct the aberrant nerve; cosmetic surgery could correct some weaknened muscles; her dilations cannot be corrected; her slight ptosis (eyelid droop) cannot be corrected without other problems developing; she will continue to have double vision. But since her mind blocks out the second blurred image "seen" by her injured eye, in actuality she is blind in one eye—and no solution for it is in sight.

This was a hard conclusion to accept, and yet we all told the Lord that if this blindness was in His plan for her we would willingly accept it from Him.

A third problem we faced was Barb's left arm. We knew that surgery would be necessary to correct the growth of bone tissue in a muscle above her elbow. Checking Barb in at the hospital on Wednesday, October 16, was rather routine. She had been in and out of three hospitals for almost six of the ten months of that year.

After the operation the next day—her 14th surgery in ten months—the surgeon explained that he had to hammer out the bone tissue with a chisel. He was encouraged, though, because her arm now had almost full movement—a range of about 135°. Over the succeeding months, it flexed open to about 155 degrees, or substantially straight.

A fourth difficulty arose—this time as a result of Barb's arm surgery. The scar from the October 17 incision began to keloid. After several visits to the plastic surgeon over several months, he concluded that plastic surgery should be performed sometime in 1976. As far as we know, this will be her final (and 15th) surgery in the long battle for recovery since her accident.

Beyond these four problems loomed a fifth and even greater burden: Would Barb have her full mental capabilities? Would her learning ability be impaired? What about her memory? Would her personality be the same?

When Barb was discharged for the first time in May, the neurologist prescribed Dilantin, a medication to be taken three times every day for at least three years. Its purpose is to help protect against the remote possibility of epileptic seizures. In addition, she must have an EEG (electroencephalogram) annually for three years. So far, the EEG's have revealed no serious problems.

Psychologically and mentally, Barb's condition is remarkable. She had a problem with short-term memory and abstract reasoning for a few weeks in the summer of 1974. At times her humor bordered on silliness. And for several months she was irritated more easily at things that did not bother her in the past. Psychological tests, however, have shown average or above average abilities in almost every area.

Tests show no evidence of any permanent personality changes or mental defects, for which we have thanked the Lord numberless times. In fact, to finish high school, Barb enrolled in a correspondence course in the fall of 1974 and completed it in three months. We were pleased with her ability to handle the course (especially considering the fact that it was physical science—not exactly her favorite subject!). Then in the spring of 1975 she enrolled in two courses at a nearby Dallas junior college, and in one course in the summer. Receiving Bs and Cs in those courses indicated that her learning ability was intact.

Her typing and shorthand skills, learned in high school, were unaffected. In fact, she typed the first draft of this manuscript, which was her own suggestion!

The fall of 1974 marked a progressive return to routine activities. In September she joined the high school youth choir of the church we attend, and for six weeks before Christmas she had a clerical job at Neiman-Marcus.

In the fall her physical therapy treatments at the hospital were reduced to once a week, and then biweekly and then monthly. By the end of 1974 they were discontinued. During the last half of the year she did several exercises at home to strengthen certain arm and leg muscles.

One day our son went to Nautilus, a physical fitness company with numerous "contraptions" and machines that strengthen many body muscles. Excited about the program, he bought a ticket admitting him to several dozen workouts. When he shared with Barb his enthusiasm for this muscle-bulging program, she wanted to try it. Now after many months of these gymnastic-like workouts, Barb's mucles have acquired remarkable stamina.

A sixth problem was financial. The hospital and surgical bills quickly climbed to several thousand dollars. Naturally I wondered how much my insurance company would pay. Again this was an area where we had to trust the Lord to meet our needs. And He did! The bills totaled more than $40,000, most of which was covered by insurance.

Still another mountain peak was before me. Dottie's physical strength was sapped and her emotional health shattered. This was especially evident in the summer when Barb's progress was stalemated. The light "at the end of the tunnel" seemed to Dottie to go out. The seemingly endless series of trachea surgeries, long days at the hospital, the haunting reminders in Barb's body of the horror of the accident, and the uncertainty of full recovery became overwhelming burdens.

Morning after morning Dottie would wake up crying. Sometimes she would cry when she went to bed. The tears were therapeutic in a sense, yet they were the outpouring of a sorrow that only a mother's tender heart can feel. They were the expression of inner pain, remorse, concern, and wishing "if only it weren't so."

True, Dottie was trusting the Lord. True, she sensed the comfort of His presence. True, she was fully aware of how God had miraculously pulled Barb back from near-death, and had brought her to a level of recovery not experienced by most patients with similar injuries. Yet her awareness of

God's presence, peace, and power did not automatically dispel the sorrow and physical exhaustion. This suggests to me that trust and grief can go together, that while a Christian is grieving he can also experience God's comfort. We "sorrow not, even as others who have no hope" (1 Thes. 4:13)—yet we sorrow.

Seeking to comfort and help Dottie was, for me, like having a second patient to care for. I tried to encourage her, to spend time with her, to take her on walks, to help with the housework.

It was difficult for Barb to understand why her mother should be so upset. "After all, look how well I am," she would tell Dottie. Then one day Dottie explained to Barb: "You have had to heal physically; I'm having to heal emotionally." That helped Barb immensely in understanding Dottie's trauma.

Though that healing process of Dottie's was slow, in time improvement was noticeable. The light brightened again and we experienced the promise of Psalm 147:3, "He heals the broken-hearted, and binds up their wounds" (NASB).

# 12

# Our Echoing Room

In the fall of 1975 Barb enrolled at John Brown University, a Christian liberal arts college in Siloam Springs, Arkansas. She is majoring in business, with an emphasis in secretarial studies.

She had been anxious for months to get started at "JB," as the students call their school. Soon after classes started she wrote to us: "I love it here! The students are all so friendly, and I like all my classes."

As my wife and I drove back to Dallas after getting Barb moved into her dorm, our emotions were surging. We were lonely—being without her company. We were anxious—wondering if she would be able to handle the school load. Yet we were also rejoicing—deeply grateful to God for restoring her physically, for retaining her mental capacities, for rejuvenating her spiritually.

Her bedroom at home, decorated in blue and

white, echoes with memories of her. Still furnished with many of her "things," it sometimes haunts us and other times stirs praise and joy. It's haunting—because it brings to mind the weeks and months in 1974 when her address was Room 947, Presbyterian Hospital, Dallas. Haunting, too, because it recalls the summer of 1974 when her room was crowded with rented medical equipment.

But the neatly arranged room, with her bell collection displayed on several shelves in a corner, is also like a chapel of praise. I pass her room several times each day, and as I do I thank God Barb is alive and well. I praised the Lord for what He has accomplished through these experiences. I worship Him for polishing our lives with the sandpaper of this trial.

As I pass Barb's room, I also pray for her. I ask the Lord to help her do well in college; to give her, in His time and plan, a fine, godly husband; to make her "grow in the grace and in the knowledge of our Lord and Saviour Jesus Christ" (2 Peter 3:18); to enable her to minister to others in *their* times of need.

Sometimes I walk into her room and the precious experiences of years past well up in my father-heart:

I think of the times when I held her, my first-born baby, in my arms.

The times when she learned to walk—and talk.

The times when I spanked her for her wrong-doing.

The times we built carrot-nosed snowmen together.

The times I watched her make mud pies and "gooshgosh" (a mixture of every kind of liquid in the house, just so she could "see what it would look like").

The times she wrote creative stories in elementary and junior high school, and signed them "Unpublished manuscript, by Barbie Zuck."

The times I helped her study high school geometry and biology.

The times when I left home for a few days on a speaking trip and she kissed me good-bye and said, "I'll pray for you, Dad."

The times when, studying the Bible, she underlined a verse and said to me, "Hey, Dad, this verse is so neat!"

The times in July 1975 when she and our son, Ken, sang radiantly with our church youth, the Phileo Singers, in their two-week, 30-concert tour of Guatemala.

The times last year when several people told her, "God must have something wonderful in store for you since He has so miraculously spared your life."

"Lord, let her furnished but empty bedroom continue to remind us—and her—of Your power to restore. Of Your ability to fill empty hearts with Your presence and joy. Of Your plan to furnish lives with purpose, praise, and peace. Of Your desire that each of our hearts be a bell of praise, chiming in tune with Your will. Amen."

# 13

# Working Together for Good

What possible blessings can come from suffering and human tragedy? Why does God permit trials that crush our bodies and souls? Like other Christians, we have found that "in all things God works for the good of those who love Him" (Rom. 8:28, NIV). These "all things," I am convinced, include so-called accidents, which in reality are incidents in God's purposes.

The following are some of the benefits that we have seen as results of Barb's "accident." Doubtless the Lord has wrought other benefits we are unaware of.

Barb's spiritual life has deepened.

Some people become embittered during severe, extended suffering. It was just the opposite with Barb. In October 1974 Barb gave a testimony in a Sunday evening church service. In part, she said, "I want to thank all of you for praying for me. I don't have any bitterness about the accident because many people are closer to the Lord." One evening in December she said to me, "I'm sorry about all that's happened this year—what it's done to you and Mom. I realize that you and Mom have been through more than I have. I wish I could have learned in an easier way not to be bitter about leaving Wheaton, but I'm not bitter now."

Barb is very much aware of God's hand in keeping her from death and in giving her a remarkable recovery. This is evident in a letter she wrote on Feb. 22, 1975, to Drs. Handley and Imaña, her brain surgeons: "When I think how I could have died or been a vegetable, God gives me peace and joy."

Three people we know of have received Christ as their personal Saviour.

Mike and Vickie, Barb's high school friends, became Christians about eight months after the accident. Barb's first "writing" (in which she asked about their spiritual welfare) and her recovery from near-death were instrumental in their conversion. How excited we were when in the fall of 1974 we heard about their salvation!

Then one Sunday evening in February 1975 Barb came home from church all excited. "Guess who is now a Christian!"

"Who?" we immediately asked.

"Layne Burgess!"

Layne was the hospital physical therapist who worked with Barb twice a day for several months.

"Really? How tremendous! How did you find out?"

"Mitzi told me tonight at church." Mitzi was a physical therapist, too, at Presbyterian Hospital. "She said Layne could not get over my speedy recovery. She had heard us say that a lot of people were praying for me and she saw God working in answer to prayer. Also, Layne was greatly impressed when I wrote to her, 'Are you a Christian?' She accepted Christ on New Year's Day."

Dottie said to Barb, "How interesting! I remember when you were becoming conscious at the end of March that you wrote, 'Are you a Christian?' to everyone who entered your room, including nurses, therapists, and friends."

Opportunities for ministry have widened.

In February 1975 I received a call from the president of the Christian Business and Professional Women's Club in Dallas. She asked if I thought Barb would be interested in speaking to their group, telling about her recovery. I said, "Frankly, I doubt it. She's never spoken to a group like that before. But you should ask her." When I got home that evening, Barb said, "Guess what? I'm going to speak to the Christian Business and Professional Women on April 21."

"Barb," I responded, "I'm surprised because I told them I doubted you would. But I'm pleased, and I know the Lord will help you in what you say."

Off and on in the next two months she planned her talk. She was not scared—till she stood up to speak. But the group cheered her on by their clapping. After the meeting many of them hugged her, rejoicing with her and praising the Lord.

I have had many occasions to share what God has

done on Barb's behalf. These have included private conversations and meetings with small and large groups. In addition, several people have asked me how to minister to friends whose loved ones were in a similar critical condition. Some of the answers I gave are included later in this book.

Many Christians have told us they have been strengthened spiritually by her recovery.

The young people at Reinhardt Bible Church, the Wheaton Evangelical Free Church, and elsewhere saw God respond in answer to their prayers. And several pastors have related to me that their congregations were united in a special way as the people prayed together earnestly for us in church services and prayer meetings.

School-age children were especially touched by Barb's need. As one example, more than a year after the accident a woman at our church told us her children still pray for Barb every day. Many adults, too, have assured us of their daily intercession on her behalf. One day a seminary student asked me how Barb was progressing, and then he remarked, "Every time I see her, I stop and stare because she is a walking miracle."

Frequently when someone has been introduced to Barb, that person has exclaimed, "Oh, I'm so glad to meet you. My family and I have been praying for you regularly."

We have learned more about the importance of prayer in the Christian's life.

When we prayed that Barb would not die in the operating room and when we prayed that she would regain consciousness and be restored, we always framed our prayers with the words "if this is Your will." Being aware of the possibility that she might not recover or be restored, we knew we were dependent on the Lord. Her health was entirely in His hands; we wanted His will done.

Therefore our prayers were for a twofold purpose: (1) to express our desires to our heavenly Father, and (2) to acknowledge our dependence on and submission to Him. Prayer is for the purpose of communing and communicating with God, not for insisting that He follow our desires. Telling God what to do would make us sovereign. In prayer the Christian should be praying for God's strength and guidance and be submitting to His will.

If we tell God what to do and He answers differently, we are disappointed and perhaps resentful against Him. But if we willingly submit in prayer to His plan for us, even when we don't know what it is, we can praise Him for sending His best. "Your will be done" is the gateway to blessing and peace of heart. "*My* will be done" is the door to disappointment and disaster.

Sometimes God answers our prayers in different ways than we expect. When I prayed in Barb's pre-accident days that the Lord would remove her bitterness, I did not expect Him to use such a traumatic or lengthy means. And when I prayed for her recovery, I did not know that the Lord would answer in a way that seemed at that time almost impossible.

The first answer demonstrated God's *authority* to do as He chooses; the second demonstrated His fabulous *ability* to do what He wishes. His authority is illustrated in Psalm 115:3, "Our God is in the heavens; He does whatever He pleases" (NASB). His ability is described in Ephesians 3:20 in that He "is able to do immeasurably more than all we ask or imagine, according to His power that is at work within us" (NIV).

Prayer, then, is the Christian's avenue of communication with the Lord to unveil his needs and concerns to Him, and to share with the Lord the desire that His will be carried out.

We have gained a fresh appreciation for hospitals and for surgeons, anesthesiologists, nurses, therapists, and ambulance drivers.

How grateful we are for the medical expertise, surgical skills, and tender nursing care of many persons in the medical profession who ministered to Barb. Our deep thanks go to the 26 doctors and surgeons, the several anesthesiologists, and the many nurses who cared for her.

Some people assume that God is not necessary if qualified medical personnel are available. After all, why should a person pray if the surgeons and nurses are competent? Doesn't the human body have recuperative powers which work whether prayer is present or not?

True, the human body has amazing curative abilities. And true, skilled medical personnel are vital. But God, who made the human body, apparently delights to help His children in response to prayer, sometimes in more dramatic ways than others, and sometimes sooner than others. Most Christian doctors do not consider themselves solely responsible for a sick person's recovery. Instead they view themselves as instruments whose knowledge and skills God can use to help restore health to the ailing or injured.

The human brain has become a fascination to me. Talking with brain surgeons and neurologists excited my curiosity, and reading books on the brain intrigued me with the revelation of its involved anatomy and extraordinary ability. This organ receives sensory signals from all parts of the body and transmits motor signals back; performs intellectual functions including memory recall, foresight, and decision-making; controls muscle movements and coordination; produces hormones linked to growth and development; and is the seat of consciousness. The physiological "wiring" of the brain's 100 billion nerve cells is highly complex and operates at mind-boggling speeds. Even without knowing these details, the psalmist accurately wrote: "Thank you for making me so wonderfully complex! It is amazing to think about. Your workmanship is marvelous" (Ps. 139:14, LB).

Our hearts have been sensitized to the physical needs of others.

Not having had any serious illnesses or hospitalizations in our family prior to Barb's trauma, I was less sympathetic and understanding of others' needs than I should have been. I like to think that one benefit of Barb's experience is a deepening of my ability to "weep with them that weep" (Rom. 12:15). As Paul wrote, the "God of all comfort . . . comforts us in all our troubles, so that we can comfort those in any trouble with the comfort we ourselves have received from God" (2 Cor. 1:3-4, NIV). I'm thankful God has sprinkled some tenderizer on my heart!

God has also used the trauma to help others in indirect ways.

Take, as an example, Merle Morris, of Wheaton, Illinois. For some time Merle had suffered a painful twitching of his eyes and a partial obstruction of his vision. He went to 16 doctors, including two psychiatrists, in a vain attempt to find relief. He could not see well enough to drive, and his employment opportunities seemed limited.

About two weeks after Barb's accident I was talking with his wife Eleanor, who works at Central DuPage Hospital. I voiced my concern for Merle and asked, "Has Merle ever gone to a neurosurgeon?"

"No," she replied. "That's one kind of doctor he hasn't seen."

"Why don't you take him to Dr. Handley, Barb's brain surgeon?" I suggested. "From what I have learned about the brain these last few days, I wonder if Merle's problem may be related organically to one or more of the nerves leading from the brain stem to his eyes."

"How could we possibly make contact with him?" Eleanor wondered.

"I'll be glad to talk with him about Merle. I'll let you know what he says."

The next day Dottie saw Dr. Handley and told him about Merle's condition. Immediately, without even seeing Merle, Dr. Handley stated the problem and said he would be glad to see him.

We relayed this news to the Morrises, and they

were ecstatic with delight. At last someone knew the problem and what to do.

A few weeks later the surgery brought marked improvement to his condition. We were pleased that the Lord had used us as a link between the Morrises and our neurosurgeon.

Another way the Lord has used Barb's recovery is to encourage medical personnel. Recently, nurses and therapists in each of the three hospitals where Barb spent some time told me that now when they have unusually difficult cases they remember Barb's situation and her recovery in the face of difficult odds.

One therapist said, "When I started working with Barb in physical therapy, I felt that her prospects for recovering to a normal condition were very slim. Now, when I may be inclined to give up other seriously injured patients who seemingly have little hope, I remember Barb. In fact, she is in my mind almost continually."

A nurse told me, "It's now two years since Barb's accident, and the staff at our hospital still talk about Barb. Our excitement about her recovery keeps us going when working with similar traumatic cases."

These benefits may be summarized in Jesus' words to Lazarus: "The purpose of his illness is not death, but for the glory of God. I, the Son of God, will receive glory from his situation" (John 11:4, LB).

One day in the summer of 1975, Barb wrote to her Uncle Keith and Aunt Ginny: "John 11:4 was written directly to me. But for lack of space, the introductory 'Dear Barb' was left off!"

Would you be ready to receive God's blessings instead of recoiling in shock and bitterness when sudden grief strikes your family? I believe Christians can develop certain attitudes to prepare them to undergo difficulties. These attitudes develop from the knowledge of biblical truths that can help you not only to endure adversity but to gain from it.

*Refuse to be surprised; don't panic.*

"Dear friends, do not be surprised at the painful trial you are suffering, as though something strange were happening to you" (1 Peter 4:12, NIV).

Face the fact now that your membership in the human race assures you the suffering of adversities. As Eliphaz said to Job, "Man is born unto trouble, as sparks fly upward" (Job 5:7).*

We are emotional beings, and adversities will inevitably cause sorrow. But the Christian's sorrow is not despair. When Paul wrote to the Thessalonian Christians about the death of saints and the prospect of the Lord's return, he said, "I would . . . that ye sorrow not, even as others which have no hope" (1 Thes. 4:13). Paul knew that along with the tears of grief can come an inner peace "which transcends all understanding" (Phil. 4:7, NIV).

*Remember God's purposes for suffering; don't be ignorant.*

The Bible mentions several purposes God has in permitting or bringing suffering into a Christian's life. Two of these reasons are purification and preparation.

---

* The Hebrew word for *trouble* which Eliphaz uses means "toil, labor, or hardship."

Some trials come to Christians as chastisement for sin. In the Corinthian church, some believers were weak and sick and others had died because of their sinful attitude toward the Lord's Supper (1 Cor. 11:27-30). Paul referred to them as being "judged" and "disciplined by the Lord" (11:32, NASB).

It is rarely possible to connect adversity with specific sin. But adversity should be an occasion for asking the Lord to reveal any sin you may not have confessed. Awareness of unconfessed sin should lead you to repentance (Prov. 28:13), and God's forgiveness (1 John 1:9).

The "silver lining" in God's cloud of chastening is the heartening truth that "the Lord disciplines those whom He loves" (Heb. 12:6, NIV). And His discipline is "for our good, that we may share in His holiness. No discipline seems pleasant at the time, but . . . it produces a harvest of righteousness and peace" (12:10-11, NIV). These benefits make far-sighted Christians appreciate their loving Father's chastening.

The wealthy King Solomon referred to the fire-refining process of silver and gold as an illustration of God's testing process: "The refining pot is for silver and the furnace for gold, but the Lord tests hearts" (Prov. 17:3, NASB). Several prophets spoke of this refining process which God used and will use on the nation Israel (Isa. 48:10; Jer. 9:7; Zech. 13:9; Mal. 3:3). And Job spoke trustingly of his suffering as a purifying process: "When He hath tried me, I shall come forth as gold" (23:10).

Gold and silver ore lose their impurities when

burned. The test demonstrates the genuine, permanent qualities. In similar fashion, trials can remove moral impurities and exhibit the faith that is genuine. "All kinds of trials . . . have come so that your faith—of greater worth than gold, which perishes even though refined by fire—may be proved genuine" (1 Peter 1:6-7, NIV).* James also said that the person who perseveres under trial is blessed because "he has stood the test" (1:12, NIV).*

Spiritual purifying produces a more stable, steadfast faith. Peter wrote that "after you have suffered for a little, the God of all grace . . . will Himself perfect, confirm, strengthen and establish you" (1 Peter 5:10, NASB). James declared a similar truth: "Knowing this, that the trying of your faith worketh patience. But let patience have her perfect work, that ye may be [mature] and entire, wanting nothing" (1:3-4). And Paul wrote, we know "that tribulation brings about perseverance; and perseverance, proven character; and proven character, hope" (Rom. 5:3-4, NASB).

Trials, then, *test* your faith as well as strengthening faith if you possess it. Many people "go to pieces" in crises because they have no personal relationship to the Saviour, and therefore no supernatural source of strength. If you do not know Christ personally, if you are not sure your sins are forgiven, I urge you to make Him your Saviour and Lord through sincere faith, "For God so loved the world that He gave His one and only Son, that whoever believes in Him shall not perish but have

* The Greek word translated "to prove" or "to demonstrate" is the same as the word translated "to test."

everlasting life" (John 3:16, NIV). "He that believeth on the Son hath everlasting life; and he that believeth not the Son shall not see life; but the wrath of God abideth on him" (3:36).

Knowing Christ as your Saviour and trusting His love and power in the face of trials, you can undergo severe testing with a calmness and peace that others cannot comprehend.

Trials, as noted in James 1:3-4 and Romans 5:3-4, produce perseverance. That is, they give Christians occasion to demonstrate a steadfast, enduring quality. The word translated *perseverance* means, literally, "to remain under." It suggests, "to hang in there," or "not to give up." Not losing heart when undergoing hardships is a means by which our character is strengthened. Thus we become more Christlike in attitude and action. Paul wrote, "For those God foreknew He also predestined to be conformed to the likeness of His Son" (Rom. 8:29, NIV).

Thinking on these biblical facts will help fortify you for difficulties you may sustain in the future. Knowing that the trials of life can be used by God to purify us, stabilize us, and strengthen us gives us an outlook entirely different from those who are ignorant of these truths. Therefore, you can say in difficult circumstances: "*What* can I get out of this?" not "*When* can I get out of this?"

God uses suffering in Christians' lives to equip them to support others in their times of need. You can more readily and fully identify with the heartaches of others when you have experienced a similar burden.

Joyce Landorf, in her book *For These Fragile Times*,* wrote of this value. The death of her young son, she said, gave her a much more responsive heart to other parents who have lost a child. It has sensitized her to be more compassionate to people in need.

Christians give substantial comfort by the few words, "Yes, I know from experience what you are undergoing." This is what Paul was speaking of to the Corinthians: "For just as the sufferings of Christ flow over into our lives, so also through Christ our comfort overflows" (2 Cor. 1:5, NIV).

*Rejoice in God's plan; don't be resentful.*

Suffering can make you better or bitter. The Bible frequently encourages Christians to rejoice in trials and to thank the Lord for them, realizing that His purposes are best.

Contemplate these verses:

"Concerning this [a thorn in my flesh, i.e. apparently some physical ailment] I entreated the Lord three times that it might depart from me. And He has said to me, 'My grace is sufficient for you, for power is perfected in weakness.' Most gladly, therefore, I will rather boast about my weaknesses, that the power of Christ may dwell in me. Therefore I am well content with weaknesses, with insults, with distresses, with persecutions, with difficulties, for Christ's sake; for when I am weak, then I am strong" (2 Cor. 12:8-10, NASB).

"And we exult in the hope of the glory of God. And not only this, but we also exult in our tribu-

---

* Published by Victor Books, 1975.

lations, knowing that tribulation brings about perseverance" (Rom. 5:2-3, NASB).

"Consider it pure joy, my brothers, whenever you face trials of many kinds, because you know that the testing of your faith develops perseverance" (James 1:2-3, NIV).

"Wherein ye greatly rejoice, though now for a little season, if need be, ye are in heaviness through manifold temptations; that the trial of your faith . . . might be found unto the praise and honor and glory at the appearing of Jesus Christ" (1 Peter 1:6-7).

These verses show that it is possible to experience true joy when you are weak, persecuted, suffering, or when you are grieving. It is not heedless gaiety nor desperate whistling in the dark, but a deep, inner serenity given by the Holy Spirit to the trusting believer.

*Rely on God's character; don't waver.*

A calm strength in storms can be experienced by Christians who contemplate the characteristics of God. Isaiah declared: "He will keep in perfect peace all those who trust in Him . . ." (Isa. 26:3, LB).

Consider the faithfulness of God. Jeremiah had pleaded with the Jewish people to abandon their sinful ways and return to God. They stubbornly refused, and therefore God sent the Babylonians to conquer their land, destroy their city, and take their people captive. Jeremiah's heart ached as he viewed the smoldering ashes of the burned city and demolished temple. The Book of Lamentations voices Jeremiah's lament over the city. He identifies himself with the city's destruction, pours out his distress, then directs his attention to God's character and ways.

"[The Lord's] compassions fail not. They are new every morning; great is Thy faithfulness. 'The Lord is my portion,' saith my soul, 'Therefore will I hope in Him.' The Lord is good unto them that wait for Him, to the soul that seeketh Him" (Lam. 3:22-25).

At first those verses seem out of place, with the Jewish nation destroyed. Yet those dire circumstances luminate God's character even more; though Judah is exiled, God will remain faithful to His people; though Jerusalem is burned, God will remain faithful to His promises; though the city is deserted, God's faithfulness is great. He is perfectly trustworthy.

Can your circumstances be beyond God's control? Hardly! Will God fail to be true to His promises to you? No! Can God go back on His Word? Indeed not!

Consider, too, the goodness of God. David declared, "I would have despaired unless I had believed that I would see the goodness of the Lord . . ." (Ps. 27:13, NASB). The supply is endless, vows Jeremiah, because His compassions "are new every morning" (Lam. 2:23). In the midst of trials, God remains good. Nahum assures us: "The Lord is good, a strong hold in the day of trouble, and He knoweth them that trust in Him" (Nahum 1:7).

God's sovereignty is another attribute that comforts us. God, the Creator of the universe, is in charge of every circumstance of your life. Knowing He is in control, Paul concluded the eighth chapter of Romans in a crescendo of praise to God's loving sovereignty.

"Who shall separate us from the love of Christ? Shall tribulation, or distress, or persecution, or famine, or nakedness, or peril, or sword? Just as it is written, 'For Thy sake we are being put to death all day long; we were considered as sheep to be slaughtered.' But, in all these things we overwhelmingly conquer through Him who loved us. For I am convinced that neither death, nor life, nor angels, nor principalities, nor things present, nor things to come, nor powers, nor height, nor depth, nor any other created thing, shall be able to separate us from the love of God, which is in Christ Jesus our Lord" (Rom. 8:35-39, NASB).

During Job's epochal trials, he apparently never knew of the heavenly dispute between Satan and God. Job was unaware that his suffering was a way of "serving" God, a means by which God was demonstrating to Satan that Job did serve Him without ulterior motives (Job 1:9). Job's endurance (James 5:11)—though he did endure at times impatiently—and his refusal to curse God demonstrated to Satan that Job's motives were pure, that he was not trading for favors.

Our trials, like Job's, may be totally unexplainable from the human standpoint, yet God may be accomplishing objectives which we will realize only in eternity. For these reasons, we do not need to insist that God explain His ways to us. To submit to the Lord in the face of bewildering adversities is the surest way of glorifying God and enjoying His peace.

Knowing of God's faithfulness—He will not let us down; God's goodness—He will always be merciful to us; and God's loving sovereignty—He is in charge and will do for us what is ultimately best in His plan, we can thank God for the trials as well as the tokens of His approval.

"As for God, His way is perfect" (Ps. 18:30).

# 14

# "How Can I Help?"

"What should I say to my friends whose child is seriously injured? In what ways can I comfort them and express my concern in a helpful way?"

Perhaps you have wanted to help someone in distress but have hesitated because you have not known what would be most suitable and appreciated. May I suggest, from our experience, some things that helped us—and mention some things that hurt? These observations may differ from the reactions of others undergoing similar crises, but some of these suggestions will help at least some of the people whom you will have opportunity to comfort, and will help you "encourage the fainthearted, and help the weak" * (1 Thes. 5:14, NASB).

* The Greek word here translated *encourage* means "to console or calm." The word *help* is also an unusual word in the Greek. It means "to keep oneself directly opposite someone, to hold him firmly, to support him." What beautiful pictures of how to assist the fainthearted and weak!

• Send cards with notes to the patient and/or his loved ones. I used to think sending a card with my signature and a Scripture verse was a sufficient expression of my concern, but receiving cards from friends during Barb's hospitalization showed me that a card which included a handwritten note of comfort and encouragement was much more uplifting.

Notice I wrote "cards," plural. Receiving a second or third card from the same friend was a guarantee of his sharing the burden. We sensed they were saying, "We are still here and concerned," and that was especially encouraging.

One seminary faculty wife continued to send cards to Barb for several months beyond the accident. They did not arrive according to any discernible pattern of time; their unexpectedness added to our and Barb's appreciation of them. An elderly woman in Wheaton, who heard of Barb's accident and introduced herself to us at the hospital still writes to Barb. These notes of love are a unique ministry carried on quietly by many of God's saints.

• Telephone the injured person's loved ones. Though some people might not care to be answering the phone frequently, I found that inquiries by telephone were encouraging. Sometimes it was easier to talk with them over the phone than in person. Phone calls, particularly during Barb's critical times, were more personal than cards or notes. Some people with a critically ill loved one want to talk because voicing the burden helps ease the load. Immeasurable support came to Dottie when a friend occasionally called her simply to say, "I love you."

• Visit the patient or his loved ones at the hospital. Of course, if a patient is in an Intensive Care Unit and only close relatives are permitted to enter, do not expect to go in unless the relative invites you and the hospital regulations allow it. If a relative asks you to see the patient (and the hospital permits it), do not hesitate to do so. But do not stay long, and comment on your concern rather than the patient's appearance. Though the patient appears unconscious he may be able to hear and remember what is said.

The presence of friends was especially supportive for us during the long surgeries. Any surgery is suspenseful because of the unknown outcome, but surgery with a higher-than-normal degree of risk, is troubling. The presence of several couples during those times was especially meaningful to us.

• Be prayerful about what you say. To us, the presence, not the sage counsel, of visitors was the most meaningful. They chatted with us about various subjects, helping to pass the time. We sensed little value in attempts to "theologize" about the purpose for this trial. We needed encouragement for the immediate moment more than speculation about the past or future.

If someone said to us, "I understand," we doubted that he really did, since he had not undergone this kind of heartache. But his saying "I'm so sorry," or "I've been praying for you," was definitely more comforting.

One well-intentioned person caused grief rather

than uplift by mentioning a relative who had died at about Barb's age. His words alerted me to avoid mentioning the death of someone else in such a situation.

Another comment that sliced like a knife into my wife's heart was a question by people who did not know our family well: "Do you have other children?" Though they sincerely wanted to know about the rest of the family, to Dottie it implied: "You have lost your daughter, who may be only a vegetable; do you have other children to compensate for this loss?" The question would be better if it were pointed clearly to the other children: "Tell me about the rest of your family."

• Help in tangible ways. Many people said, "Let me know if I can help." They meant well, of course, but of greater help were those who offered specific assistance.

One example: "We want to bring you your supper. Would tomorrow night or the next night be better?"

Preparing a meal for the family of a hospital patient may not seem to be much help, but it is a highly appreciated load carrier. For months Dottie found it difficult because of her tired physical condition to prepare meals for Ken, herself, and me. Picking up the dishes afterward or using disposable dishes avoids the addition of one more chore. You can render a wonderful, loving service by preparing a meal for a family in such need; we know what this means!

Some gave us money, knowing we would have additional financial needs at that time. Still others made known their loving support by thoughtful gifts—a planter, a book, a basket of fruit.

Others expressed their love by sending Barb artificial flower arrangements and stuffed animals. She especially enjoyed the autograph Snoopy dog, which she asked friends, nurses, and therapists to sign. Nurses at Central DuPage Hospital, hearing of Barb's recovery, purchased an autograph book, signed it, and mailed it to Barb.

Giving us a Scripture verse typed on a 3″ by 5″ card was yet another way of offering encouragement.

As mentioned in an earlier chapter, numerous people sat with Barb at the hospital both before and after she regained consciousness. They insisted on coming each week for two or three hours at a time, thus relieving us of an endless vigil. When Barb was fully conscious, she enjoyed people coming to talk with her and to play Scrabble with her. Since her recovery, people have asked her, "Wasn't it a bore spending all that time in the hospital?" She assured them it wasn't because of the many people who spent time with her.

• Ask what specific needs you can pray for. Knowing that people were interceding for Barb's particular needs was more encouraging to us than general prayer support. And God answered in response to specific prayer burdens. For example, not long after several people prayed for Barb's left eye, it began to open. Others, after praying for her left arm, were thrilled to see her move it.

Prayers by God's people recorded in the Bible were specific. Ours should be too. Therefore you can help by asking a patient or the relatives what needs you can pray for. Indeed, "The prayer of a righteous man is powerful and effective" (James 5:16, NIV).

Yes, if you love you can help.

# 15

# Sincerely, Barb

I am deeply thankful to God for saving me from death and for healing me completely. I realize how close I came to dying and to being impaired in some way for life.

Through this experience God has taught me the importance of letting Him handle all situations in my life. Once I learned to trust Him in a few areas, it became easier to hand Him others. I have also learned what a Friend He is. After I became conscious and was still in the hospital I often talked with the Lord in prayer. What a comfort it was to know that He was always near me even when visiting hours ended in the evenings.

I am grateful to so many people. First, I thank my parents and my brother for sticking by me, praying for me, and working with me in the hospital week after week. I realize now that they went through more heartache than I did. Also thanks to the many doctors, nurses, and therapists who took such personal interest in my "case." And thanks to the many friends and others—whom I had not previously met—for their acts of kindness.

I pray that as you have read this book the Lord has spoken to you and that you have seen how powerful and loving He is, and how important it is not to go your own way, but to trust Him in simple faith. As my dad has said, "In God's plan there are no accidents, only incidents."

Sincerely,
Barb